MW01657191

Love
Marty

My Sister Has Lived a Nightmare

by
Martha Ulrich

DORRANCE PUBLISHING CO., INC.
PITTSBURGH, PENNSYLVANIA 15222

ISBN # 0-8059-3780-3
Printed in the United States of America

First Printing

For information or to order additional books, please write:
Dorrance Publishing Co., Inc.
643 Smithfield Street
Pittsburgh, Pennsylvania 15222
U.S.A.

Table of Contents

History Repeats Itself

This is the true story of Mickey—an abused wife for forty-five years. I am bringing it out in the open.

Mickey and Dan were living in a mobile home after selling out the big homestead. Now that was stress, living daily with surveyors. Retirement was supposed to be a time to relax and start enjoying their lives; what a crock of shit that turned out to be. Her husband had retired and they were at a time in their lives when the golden years were setting in.

Dan's favorite position was sleeping in the recliner he bought for his wife. It was supposed to help her back; that was so she could keep her nose to the grindstone and to keep her in shape so she could cook her homemade pies, cookies, and cakes to feed Dan. Mickey had to take good care of her man so the man that calls himself a bastard would stay healthy, and the instigators he called his friends could persuade him to go out to their parties, hang in barrooms, feed him beer, and rape their wives. They sent him home to the wife drunk, so he could smash up furniture, or any choice possession in the house of hers, then stalk off to bed.

When he got up the next morning, the King needed his coffee. He didn't have time to discuss problems of the day; he was too hungover and tired from his little fling with another woman. He was depressed; he had something on his dirty old mind. He told his wife the reason he didn't have sex with her was that she didn't turn him on. He expected Mickey to hug and kiss him and forgive him because, in one of his weaker moments while at the party he found a slut that was just so sexy he couldn't resist her. Dirty old man. I hope they enjoyed it.

Mickey had locked the door so she could get some rest. With the King gone, at least she could get some rest from his complaining—and would you believe she could have the full-size bed for a change? It was a Christmas present from a few years back; he allowed her to pick it out. I'm surprised he didn't bring his slut home and ask Mickey to go into another room so she could listen to their heavy breathing while they got it on. No, he was much too kind; he would sneak it and hope she didn't find out.

The first thing Mickey heard when she awakened from her sleep was good old Dan with a crowbar, trying to break into the mobile home. He couldn't wait to get into the King's bed; he was so exhausted from his friend's retirement party. Dan always made sure to tell her what a nice time he had without her and that nobody asked where she was. He would rub her and ask her how long it'd been since she hugged him. What did she expect? He must have spent at least two hours with her that day; that would ease his conscience. He always slept well, being tired from his little flings. He probably told the slut to keep her mouth shut so the wife wouldn't find out. Isn't that the way a good husband and outstanding man of the community plays his little game? Wife, woman, mother were his loving names for her—what more did she want?

He had finally started doing the dishes and making the bed after forty-four years of marriage. Now he deserved a night out. Nice guy, the neighbors thought; the little mouse that lived under the bed in the house went hee-hee.

The naive wife got up to let her husband in so the door wouldn't get broken apart. She had to keep the trailer in good shape; then he'd let her sell it as long as she took all responsibility for having it moved, paid for the moving, and did all the groundwork for having it moved. Then he wanted his half when it was sold so he could get a divorce and make an honest woman of the slut that enticed him, and, being so weak, he didn't want to hurt her feelings so he met her wishes. That was the way old Dan expected life to be. Why not? His father got away with it; his mother covered for him. Why shouldn't Mickey do it for him?

Wrong Dan; Mickey is not your mother. It's about time you answer for your own weakness—women. How much could a wife swallow?

He said he didn't screw shit. We'll see. She (the other woman) couldn't hide in the shadows forever. I hoped it wasn't some young girl. A relative? Mickey, you never know. I'm sure Dan told her how badly his wife treated him. That is usually the man's cop-out, and the dumb broad fell for it. Whoops, Dan just got pleasure from raw sex. If his wife couldn't accept that that is the way men are, that's her problem. He wanted to tell Mickey how men are?

I think she learned from her father who accused our mother of seducing every man that entered their home until it became a family joke amongst the seven children: Which neighbor was their father? Sick! Jealousy!

He lived in the barn more than in the home. That was after we would wake every morning to wonder if we would find our mother dead. Then the fun really began. Mickey and our sisters and brothers would run down the winding stairs with the little snowdrifts on the steps, missing the curve a few times, and sliding down the rest of the stairs on their backs. We would throw open the door to find no breakfast. We were too late; the grape jelly and fried eggs were already sliding down the freshly papered walls.

It was time to drive Old Cotton Ears out. We had a father with a dirty mouth. The best ammunition was the four quart manger sitting on the counter. Ginger was the best shot; she laid one right between his eyes. She had a dead eye for Old Shark Tooth; I can see it yet: Father running around in his rubber boots ready to go milk the cows and beat the horses with the iron milk stool. I suppose that was how he got his vengeance out. He stayed there for at least a week before he would worm his way back into Mother's bed, living on home-rendered lard and salt and pepper; that was his favorite food. Polish sausage? He would throw that across the table, yelling "Pig's nuts!" Maybe he was right. You never know. Those were the temper tantrums of a grown man. Never allowing the children to laugh at the table, he would slap us across the mouth if we complained about any food served. He told us we would shit a slimmer turd.

Mickey was his favorite. He would give her a dime to sweep the barn. She'd roll his cigarettes on the little canvas cigarette machine, Bugler being the favorite brand. So many for Dad, so many for Mickey. She would comb his hair with a fine-toothed comb, always wanting him to love her, but he was too busy listening to the battery-operated radio, absorbed in his world. One of the nicer things he did was to bring home a gas lantern with those two little balls that when lit gave us more light than kerosene lamps. We had made a move up. Now we could play cards more easily; we could actually see the numbers on the cards. That was about the only enjoyment there was then.

We would grab a pitcher and go down into the cellar. It had a dirt floor, of course, and you would hope you wouldn't have a few rats run over your feet. We would take a flashlight because we had to be careful not to fall over the deer that Old Shark Tooth had killed so we could eat for another day. Those were the good old days: Popcorn made in the old frying pan and simmered in bacon grease; that still tastes good. When we went to bed we slept four in a bed with the old double flannel sheets. It kept the four of us warm, one boy and three girls. We weren't allowed to laugh then either or he would threaten to turn the lights out. Soon we had moved up another notch and had an electric drop cord with a bulb hanging on it, fly shit being its decor.

We would get up in the middle of the night, crawl out of the little window over the stairs, and watch the little stream of pee run down the roof. Mickey would lay in bed and cough up pinworms in chunks and throw them on the floor. She probably ate too many of the beautiful spice apples.

That was the part of Mickey's life that was full of pleasure. She would jump on the old swayback chestnut mare and go and get the cows. Nanny Goat always led the herd; they were not purebreds by any means, just a conglomeration of whatever could be bought or traded as producers of milk. Mickey would milk Holsteins at four each morning and each night at our sister's farm. That was before milking machines. As long as they had long teats you learned how to pull and squeeze. The rich foam built up on the big galvanized pail amidst the smell of the cows. Holsteins produced more milk; Guernseys and Jerseys gave richer milk. Now we could use a separator to separate the cream from the milk.

When it was time to make butter, we would take a gallon jug filled half full and use a crank handle with a cover that screwed on top of the jug with four wooden paddles. We would start turning the handle—the milk had to be room temperature—and when the little yellow flecks started showing up, you knew the butter was ready to be formed in a wooden bowl. With the wooden paddle you would press it to get all the buttermilk out and add a little salt. No commercial butter ever tasted so good. The buttermilk was the remaining juice and also had a flavor that no big time operation could copy.

For cottage cheese from soured milk, clobbered was the name for it, we would put it in a clean pillowcase, tie a string around it, and hang it on the clothesline. Once all the juice dripped out, we had cottage cheese in all its glory.

Hams hung in the old storeroom. We had layer after layer of pork loins fried and preserved with grease, fricasseed chicken with biscuits and gravy, homemade pies, cakes from scratch, and Dutchman's fried bread dough. While it was warm, we had to punch a few holes into it with a fork to let the fresh butter melt through the holes—you thought you had died and gone to heaven.

Were those days so bad? I think not. Saddle shoes, wool socks, the Depression of 1929, they were poor times. Kids considered it playing to pick bushel after bushel of green beans. If you got dropped off a mile from the blackberry patch, you had better not come out before your milk pail was full of the biggest, juiciest berries. Of course you could always feed your face and gobble a few, so you didn't need to carry a lunch. We learned to eat leeks, and fried little red potatoes after they had been boiled and peeled. Kids at school would ask what in hell we had been eating. Of course we couldn't smell our breath, and as long as everyone ate the same things, who cared? That's the spirit of youth.

Welfare dresses came in about that time; they were green with brown trim. If you were lucky, they were brown with green trim, or you could wear the ones your mother stayed up half the night to sew. Mickey was told she looked like a bag of rags tied in the middle by her favorite boy in school—compliments, compliments, they were a dime a dozen. she took it with a grain of salt, chasing Vince down the street; poor little guy, he had three girls after him while he yelled.

As for games, kick the can, three sticks, and pom-pom were far and away the favorites. With hide-and-go-seek, Skip, Mickey's dog, always sniffed her out so she was first to be found. Mickey found Skip when the little poodle dog wandered into the yard. Mickey brought it a piece of bread or a piece of meat when no one was looking, petted it, and loved it. At night Old Shark Tooth would beat the little dog with a stick until it would leave. Finally Skip didn't come back. Mickey stayed in the house and cried. About that time, Mickey's sister, Capitola, started dating. Unbeknownst to anyone, Capitola's boyfriend brought Mickey her first dog from his dog's litter. She hid it under the covers in her bed, only bringing it out when no one was around. She would feed it, take it outside, train it, and put it back under the covers until it was safe to sneak it out again. That lasted about a week, until she was finally allowed to keep it.

Mickey learned fast. When all of the other kids were getting the belt for coming home late from riding bikes, she would hide in the closet, listening to them get their well-deserved smack with the leather belt, and then, crying, she would come out to join them.

Brother Bud and Mickey had their first swimming lesson in the old creek. They had walked a mile toting the old inner tube in their sunsuits; there were no bathing suits. Mickey tried to flip Bud; he grabbed her by the ass, ripping a big hole in her only sunsuit. Mickey walked that mile home indifferent to pride; there were no cars on the road anyhow, just Bud and Mickey trying to get home on time knowing full well the belt was waiting. Mickey hid in the closet, letting Bud take the beating this time; after all he was always Ma's favorite. She loved him the best. Mickey never could figure out why.

Mickey was the middle child; she got the leavings from the older and younger siblings and had a spirit no one could break. Today she would be labeled a strong-willed, hyperactive brat. Mickey considered what her mother must have gone through with seven children all clamoring for attention; there was no birth control then. It was a time of dry births, scrubbing boards, Fels Naphtha Soap, and lean years—not a time for living high on the hog.

Mickey named the old woodshed Schopper's Shit Hole. The people who had lived there before our family moved in had used it wherever a board was missing. This was not the style of our family. We had a two-seater that was emptied and limed regularly to keep the flies away. Next to the seat were catalogs from which Mickey picked out the dresses and shoes she knew damn well she would never get. Those little red velvet slippers with a metal bar jabbing her in the foot that came from a grab bag from the neighbors were her favorite possessions for all of one summer.

Mickey loved getting her first job, housework after school for two dollars each week. There were two kids to watch; their messy diapers were often rubbed into a screened crib and left for Mickey to clean, and she had to vacuum the rugs on her hands and knees with a little car vacuum cleaner. Still it was better than at Mickey's house.

At home she dropped onto linoleum floors, her favorite pets were a litter of newborn mice she had found when tipping over the corn shocks. At home there were boxes from oil stove wicks, batten from worn-out quilts, and two-quart green canning jars with zinc tops. Those were the toys of the good old days. Baby rabbits wrapped in a blanket were sure to be sat on by someone before the day ended. Our brother was into raising bantam chicks then. One day Mickey jumped off the steps and landed on one of those cute little chickens. Her brother was screaming that she had squashed the guts right out of him; his little gizzard slid out. It made Mickey get a sick feeling in the pit of her stomach. She would never kill an animal on purpose. She loved the animals. This was just another accident on the farm.

One night old Redbone Coon Dog lay with a cast on his leg on the kitchen floor where he had just peed. After he had gulped down about five baking powder biscuits, he was then thrown the old dishrag which he was smart enough to hack out.

A normal day would include driving the tractor for Old Shark Tooth when he would call Mickey a few choice names. It was a new farm tractor and she was seven years old and didn't know the brakes should be locked. More choice names flew from Old Shark Tooth's mouth so Mickey told him where to shove his tractor, and she guessed it wouldn't fit, but "mean old son of a bitch" was running through her head. He had lost his driver.

Old Shark Tooth had a hearing problem. "Huh?" was his favorite response to anything Ma said. As he walked through the kitchen one day, Mickey barely whispered, "Cotton Ears!" Suddenly, his hearing was sharp; he spun around in what seemed like one giant step and left his finger marks across her mouth. She guessed she deserved that.

Today Mickey thinks of those times and the theory that we marry a mate similar to our father. Not intentionally, she thought. While she was young, naive, and looking for something better than home, Mickey fell into the trap of marriage believing that if she was a good and faithful wife with the education from home, and as part of a new generation, her marriage would be different—wrong. The men in Mickey's husband's family were raised by a father who tried every woman he could, including Mickey, because he figured as long as his son picked her he might as well share her. Keep it in the family? As long as you won't tell! Dysfunctional is a new name for a dirty old man.

Mickey got the product of such a home. Dan never would stand up to his father for her. Nobody ever told; they swept it under the carpet. Would she keep family secrets? No way! Mickey ratted on the old bastard, waiting in fear in the upstairs apartment for a couple of years for the next time. She didn't talk to him for a few years. Her kids learned to call him Grampa, but he didn't change. He put Mickey's two little girls in the bathtub when Grandma was trusting him to baby-sit. If Mickey would have known she probably would have killed the dirty old man. Family members didn't want this known. Where did Dan get his education? It wasn't out behind the barn! They figured these were men's rights. Well, it was about time it was exposed. It might have saved some other girl from falling into the same trap.

Then Dan pulled the same crap! He cheated, became divorced, and blamed everything on the wife. He thought he should make an honest woman out of his prey. Mickey felt sorry for him but couldn't back down. Finally she turned him in to the sheriff's department, which was not much help, and to the town judges, who were not much help either. He would do anything for Mickey if she didn't blow it out. I think he only had himself to blame that time. Not dealing with his mother, hurting his wife, children, and grandchildren, what would he get away with next? The sheriff's department wanted to use him as an example. Mickey contemplated calling the paper and letting them get more information to publish. She wondered what excuse Dan would make. You know how weak men are! That's no excuse. He could have had the same control his wife had. Weak? Weakness of character is more like it.

I just took a hike down to the pond; I had to clear my mind. It's an overcast evening. The fish are jumping, and the peepers are singing. It's spring in Wales, and the daffodils are just starting to peep their yellow wings out like baby chicks.

Now back to Mickey; where was I? Oh yeah, Easter Sunday arrived, sunny and beautiful, and we went to church; what a refreshing experience. The singing and the organ playing hallelujah, hallelujah, brought a serenity to Mickey. Tears were running down her face as she tried to get through an Easter Sunday, finding contentment for an hour and a half sitting on the soft blue seats, watching other people hurting with heavy hearts searching for their God, and wanting him to take the pain of life away; pain which was usually caused by another human being.

Some people could be so cruel; they use their vicious tongues on other people to try and make themselves look good. Mickey wondered why. Should she have to excuse them or forgive them; that is the sickness in the society today. It is a dog eat dog world, but it doesn't work. Cheating on wives? It doesn't work. Latchkey children? It doesn't work. What about divorces and lawyers trying to grab some money from someone else's pain? Some of them are so cunning they try to twist every word in order to make the one who has done wrong look like a nice person. No, the law says everyone is entitled to a defense. What about the one who called the wife who didn't commit adultery? People slander her every time she goes out in public. If she dances with someone, she hears, "Who is that, your stud?" These words come from a young punk on drugs who is drinking and has an illegitimate baby who is wondering why he was conceived—where does this end?

The devil made him do it? I don't think so. That is an excuse for sick human beings, an excuse for their own weakness. That's reality? That's the way men are? That's a COP-OUT in capital letters. I goofed? No, they think it is their right—Wrong! They lost control. They have no respect for their wives or any women; they're all alike!

Years ago they beat their women with clubs; Dan used his dirty mouth on his wife, and his so-called friends backed up his sick behavior. They were as sick as he was. The kids watched his behavior and thought it was alright—Wrong!

Each generation thinks they will change the world—Wrong! A human being never changes from generation to generation. They hurt emotionally from another's wrongdoing, and eventually the conscience of the wrongdoer starts eating away at his brain. He takes it out on his wife and tries to make himself look good in the eyes of the world, so he knocks the wife in public and thinks that will build his ego—Wrong! It just makes him look like the piece of shit he really is.

Grandchildren become warped from the dirty mouths, actions, and wrongdoing of parents. One of the sayings whispered to Mickey was, "Your grandson isn't worth the come that ran down your daughter's leg." God that made her sick. How could a father say he loved his son and make that kind of remark about him? Who raised that little boy? What do you expect from such teachings? He had such low self-esteem. What could a grandmother say that would erase those feelings? It was best not to tell him. He had been put down enough and was not praised enough in the home. The bad thing was that the grandmother kept her mouth shut for years to keep peace in the family—Wrong! That didn't work either. There were no answers, so she tried to live with it. She loved the children through it; hugged and kissed those grandchildren, and let them know it was not their fault. The only advice she could give them was to turn it around. From everything they didn't like about the home in which they were raised, they could turn it around and try to not make the same mistakes. None of us will every be perfect; we are also imperfect human beings.

Finally, when we get old enough to have the wisdom, our children do not want to listen. So they fall into their own buckets of shit, only to find out that their parents were not perfect; nobody handed them the golden book of rules on parenting either. However, if they were given the basics—discipline, good food, a mom who would discipline them and would be waiting there when they came in the door with the smell of the beef roasts cooking and molasses cookies warm from the wood stove oven, clean clothes, a hug when they bruised their knees, a Christmas tree with twinkling lights, the time to solve their problems, a father and a mother—what more could they expect? Not to appreciate that is. Ask anyone who was cheated of this. Go back to the family traditions; family reunions—those are the good memories: the kids with their innocence and curiosity, trying to learn from the older people, trying to weave their way through life and parents wondering if they gave them enough strength to get through life, knowing that is not always going to be easy.

Accepting death is the hardest part of life, trying to believe that those people are waiting for us on the other side, knowing there is no escaping it, never having that answer until it becomes reality, and wondering how we accept it. Knowing it will happen eventually, not when we humans would chose it, allows us to know that someone greater than ourselves is in control of this universe. We are just puppets playing a role and enjoying life until God pulls our strings and whispers: "Come back to Me; I have something better waiting for you. You have been hurt enough; I am walking right beside you. You have never been alone; I love you, I created you, I like you just the way you are."

After Five Months of Separation!

Separate living. Shelly Rhulen from domestic violence hadn't called back after three days to let Mickey know when the next court date was to take place. The article looked good, but that is not much help when you are living in terror and fear daily!

Dear Dan,

Your irrational behavior on the phone last night is just going to get you in more trouble. I called our daughter Candy after talking with you on the phone and asked if she had the stapling gun; she said no. She returned it to you and said you acted alright Sunday morning when she called you. She wonders why you would tell the constable that I live like a pig while you were at our place picking up your saw and personal papers. Guess you'll have to explain that to her yourself.

You were given permission to come to the house, and look how you abused it. What's wrong with you? If you threaten to have the electric and phone shut off you will just bring more trouble on yourself. By dropping charges, I'm the only one that can keep you out of jail, which I would have done if you would have accepted help from anyone. The more you act foolish and swear at me and accuse me of sleeping with other men, the easier it makes it to let the law prevail.

When I talked to Dr. Ruben about you, after I made the appointment for you before leaving for the Cleveland Clinic to see if I could get help for my back problem, I couldn't believe he did not send you for a brain scan to see if there was something physically wrong with you or test you for Alzheimer's Disease to find out what is at the bottom of your problems. It's hard to tell what's wrong with you as your irrational behavior isn't getting any better. He could give you some medication if it is depression as you told me you had. You have to talk to him about it—you are certainly not yourself. Your uncontrollable rage is not like you.

Love,
Mickey

Continuation of letter to Dan

The next time you see your landlord, tell him how you had divorce papers served on your wife on her sixty-second birthday. Brag about letting her do all the work on the lawn, planting trees and shrubs, and having to ask a neighbor boy to help her. Tell him about making her pay the mortgage on your new home while you were out working to pay your lawyer for the divorce without telling her so she could hear it on the answering machine when playing back messages, as if you didn't know it was recording your conversation, before the mortgage papers were signed. Be sure to tell him how you threatened to have a sheriff take her to the bank and force her to sign after you harassed her all morning about signing and how you came out of your sick room in the garage and spit a big slimy mouthful of spit at her when she came outside to paint on the concrete statues you ordered so you could sell the house and get your half out of it. Tell him you expect her to stay here and look after a faulty furnace that you had put in the house, which you could not afford, while you withhold support money from her to live on. And tell him how you expect her to pay for fixing the furnace on her meager income and see how long he will want you for a tenant.

This is what I had spoken to the doctor about, and he wanted to know if you were crazy. Why don't you go to him and tell him yourself? Ask for help. He could steer you in the right direction. You have to be a man enough to go ask for help and not expect your wife to do it for you. If you can't remember what you acted like take this letter to Dr. Ruben's and show it to him. Your sickness went to Cowlesville with you. What would you think if I accused you of stealing the stapling gun after you bought it? Or what about accusing me of stealing your clothes out of your sick room when I was trying to find out if you still had keys to the house, especially when you said you had given them to me so you couldn't go after me again?

The people from domestic violence with whom I have been working asked me, "My God, Mickey, how did you put up with this for so long? If Dan was any kind of a man, he would just give you the house for all you have done for him for forty-five years. You deserve that and more." Is this what you want me to lie about for you, Dan? I'm not going to cover up for you; saying this is the way men are is no excuse.

I looked at you in court last night as you walked in; I thought it might shame you into getting help. Did it? Take this letter to court; tell the judge how you accuse your wife of going all over men in a barroom if she sits in a booth with one talking, and ask him if he thinks you have problems. Why don't you take a good look at yourself in the mirror? What do you see? The reflection of what I have been living with for quite some time. Not a pretty picture, is it? It won't bother me one bit if you read this letter out loud in court.

Mr. O'Malley knows I went to the restaurant where you and my supposed friends were eating to demand some money from you so I could keep up with expenses. Everyone I have told says, "Good for you, Mickey; it's about time you stand up for yourself." How dare I embarrass you in public? If you were any kind of a man, you would have told Sherry and Dean to keep out of our business and that it is between you and me instead of asking me to leave since I wasn't wanted there. Still think you are better than I? Mr. O'Malley, the lawyer, laughed and wanted to know if I got some money? Yes, I shamed him into sending me 300 dollars after waiting a month and a half. Darwin told me he still wants to be my friend—fine, fine friend. He and his wife are taking you out to eat, shows me what kind of people they are. I don't need their kind of friendship. He hasn't called me since. If his wife likes to be called a fucking bitch that is up to her; I don't care to work for those wages anymore. Too bad you and Lee were embarrassed. I felt that way for years when you made your nasty remarks about me in public. Neither of you have the right to look down your nose at me, in public or anywhere else. We are all equal human beings. Too bad I had to go that far so that people know what kind of family I have. I can't change any of you, but I don't have to allow you to run my life nor do I have to accept your bad manners. If you were embarrassed, you asked for it. Most people know better than to pull that kind of crap you do.

The day you came out of the garage and treated the men from the security company the way you did embarrassed me. They told me not to let it bother me and to forget it; they had seen your kind many times, and they drove away laughing at you. They thought you were a crazy old coot. That's what your uncontrollable behavior is doing for you. This is the way Henry Meyers acted. The doctor told Jean he has mental problems. His son Butch keeps him in line.

You ask me why I don't wear my negligees to the door like other women do? Because I would have to fight off men with their dirty minds, and I have never had to; I have been pushing them away for years, self-respect and marriage being my standards. Guess you never appreciated a wife like that. I didn't care to be manhandled by everyone that came to the door. I'm still getting lots of offers, but I consider the source. I respect married women who don't want to run around with married men whose place is home with their wives, just as you should have been.

Taking over some of the household chores wouldn't hurt you. You retired from your job. I would like to retire from some of my duties also and have more leisure time to do things I enjoy doing.

You choose divorce if you do not get your own way; you take up with another woman. You play your games with Candy when I'm at work then yell when I walk in the door from work after five hours of dealing with the public, after doing three hours work before I go on the job. I have to put up with some nut driving side by side with me down Centerline Road on my way home from work. He almost ditched me that night and was standing by the car in the garage when I got out of the car with the excuse that he needed directions; then I have to be confronted by you telling me to ask Correne from work to stop annoying you by calling on the phone which I didn't know anything about. That is a little much. I can hear it now: What if I would have staggered in the door drunk, puked in the toilet for two hours, then fell on the floor with my pants around my ankles like I have watched you do many times?

These are the memories the kids have of their father—not all of them. They also remember their mom running to kiss their dad when he came in the door from work. Playing the dutiful wife, Mickey had a good meal simmering on the wood stove, and she always looked like a million bucks because the King had arrived home. Not really. This was her idea of how a wife should treat the man when he came home. That was after she dumped the ashes from the wood stove that she had baked those tempting molasses cookies in after the chimney had burned out, almost burning the house down. As the paper scorched around the chimney, we grabbed rags and slapped them on the paper; it worked.

The reservoir on the side of the stove warmed the water to do the dishes as all there was in the kitchen was the pitcher pump and the old blue sink. That was after graduating from the upstairs to the downstairs apartment in their in-laws' house. That was even worse—a three-burner oil stove and a sink in a storeroom with no heat and which could only be cleaned if the door was left open long enough to warm the grease and scum when enough heat was generated by the stovepipe from the coal stove in the downstairs living room. That storeroom also contained the white porcelain pot which served as a potty break in the middle of the night.

This was 1948, and things were looking up with two little girls to take care of. They would carry their blue granite pot downstairs and dump it in Grandma's toilet. She was rich and had a flush toilet and, would you believe, a bathtub. Wow! The Depression in 1929 was still around.

They were living high on the hog then. It was hilarious when Grandma came up to visit Mickey one day—it was a daily thing—and told her she heard the damnedest noise in the middle of the night. Would you believe her prodigal son had come home drunk, and slapped six-month-old Terry on the butt because he had woken her up stumbling around while trying to get undressed? He was drunk again; also drunk last night and drunk the night before. "Gonna get drunk like I never got drunk before" was his going thing. When he put his head over the bed to puke, Mickey raised up and told him to clean it up. I laugh as I write this. Her memory was so vivid as she recalled Dan grabbing his ass, jumping out of bed, and grabbing some newspaper. I'll tell you, that damn linoleum really had a shiny spot about three feet in diameter the next morning; that was after he went flying into the good old faithful storeroom on his hands and knees trying to make the pot. It beat the hell out of diving out the window of The Wolf House (their honeymoon cottage).

He never told Grandma and neither did Mickey. Would she have believed them? Not her fair-haired, conceited snob, as he was known as on the school bus. Would she have believed he had ripped off two buttons from Mickey's seersucker suit the first time he took her home from Griffin Mill's square dance? Mothers have a hard time believing their boys reach puberty and will do the same things dads do. So why tell them?

Dan bragged about him and his friend catching skunks all week in their convertible with the rumble seat then dating the girls. He would also rip open the box of Kotex and make fun of Mickey because she wore them. That was a move to moderation. Older girls wore flannel rags and washed them. That's where the slang word used by the boys came from then: "Don't take her out tonight; she is ragging." No one talked about having a period or menstruation; that was a "no." And if the girl got pregnant, she was a whore while the boy walked away and whistled a happy tune; he scored. If you wore a maternity suit, you were bragging. Times have changed.

We were so damn poor Mickey would have killed just for a peanut butter sandwich unlike those damn rich kids in school, which was a "one roomer" and held eight grades. The teacher had halitosis, was hungover, and beat poor Bernadette over the back with a geography book until she was under the desk. She used a rubber hose for the boys and would take them in the entry. Frank came in crying; "It didn't hurt, but I've got a headache" were his words.

The old backhouse served for two purposes: expelling human waste and telling dirty jokes. It was also the favorite thing to tip over on Halloween. Our father would sit in the kitchen and shoot through the screen door, but it was always horizontal by morning. It was a good time to clean it anyhow; lime being the only disinfectant. Was it so bad? It was better than polluting the ground with Saniflush or the likes which might stay in the ground for years.

Mickey learned easily. She and her girlfriend, two in a class, skipped third grade; both learned while other classes were being taught. The teacher wanted them to also skip fourth but Mother said no, a word now forbidden with children.

It is a new generation. This is the generation of drugs, divorce, and AIDS; you name it. Who is to say? I think the '40s, '50s, and '60s were pretty good years. Apple bins in the cellar were filled with Northern Spice, Hubbarsons, Baldwins, and Wagoners. These were apples that would keep all winter without cold storage since the cellar was the "Fridge." The smoked hams and bacon were in the cellar as were home canned tomatoes.

Mickey could ride a horse bareback to get the cows at eight years of age. The horse was usually an old swayback which was bought for twenty dollars at the Springville auction where the farmers took day-old calves or any animal that was to be sold. Mickey's father bought her a black calf to raise and told her it was hers. However the day came when that was sold also. He would get a horse and beat it with iron milk stools, trying to break its spirit, and when the animal was hurt, he would ask her to see if she could get in the stall by the horse. She would pet the horse and rub its side and walk in the stall. It taught her to love the animal and gain confidence. She still loves the animals. She reversed the treatment her father gave to animals; turned it completely around. She showed that love works on anything which has been beaten either spiritually or physically.

Now she is trying to get herself together from physical and verbal abuse from the man she married. Her hands shake everyday, and she is smoking too much. Too much is hanging on her again: financial stress and a husband who is withholding support and refuses to talk like an adult on the phone. He slams the phone down in her ear if she calls him or gives her five minutes to talk, then absorbs three of those minutes with his arguing until she tells him to shut up.

The reality is that Dan is a double of the father in Mickey's childhood. She goes to Al-Anon meetings every Monday in a church basement. There she gets hugs and emotional support; she tries to gain strength so that she can make it through another week. She also goes to counseling to try to get some of the hurt out that is buried deep inside. She is hiding the hurt from her children and friends, wondering if it will ever stop.

Some help is being offered from an oversexed Indian who has fallen in love with her. However, he is married and has a sick wife but would like to supply Mickey with sex or whatever her desires are. Her answer is, "I'm on the shelf; I'm just not ready to allow myself to get hurt again." Also her standards are not to mess with married men. It would be so easy to give in to meet the needs that are dying to be met. She is a woman who loves sex but who has been deprived by her husband. At the same time she can picture him with another woman getting his needs met. It stirs such mixed emotions of hate and loathing, but she is trying to accept it all and forgive it, knowing that he is one sick man.

She has detached herself from the problem by learning to play the electric organ on her own. It amazes her that she can do this by taking time to sit down an put her hands on the keys. Playing the organ has been one of her goals of life. Mickey always loved music, dancing, and singing; God blessed her with many talents. Still she is hungry for human companionship; she is lonely and feels very misunderstood. Mickey goes to a small restaurant on Friday nights where she might have one drink. As the designated driver, she switches to cranberry juice; she might have a fish fry and she chitchats with the bartender. He is very neat and doesn't tell anyone's secrets. She likes that. With a big grin on his face, while he blends bloody marys or whatever the customers order, he says he has virgin eyes. There might be other divorcees to chat with, all facing the same heartaches and trying to fill the hours, the empty void that the drinks won't fill. It's either that or return to an empty house, wondering how or what direction to take in life to level out.

If you try to share what is happening to you, you will constantly hear that they don't want to hear it or they don't want to get involved. But you know inside that they really can't solve the problem; you have to.

Being a woman, Mickey knows what she needs and wants to survive: many hugs, understanding, kisses, and someone to squeeze her hand and help her regain confidence. She needs to learn to trust human beings with their vicious tongues rather than wanting to be criticized or put down for everything and the actions she takes. She is a fallen person; she is at loose ends, but she is trying to get it together again. It's scary for her, never knowing if she will be able to go to work to help the financial problems.

She waited for help for four months. Dan was supposed to supply her with money for fuel bills, but his excuse was that he was behind and short of help. One blessing was that summer was close. She could try to do wood crafts, make Easter candy, rent the camper, sell the trailer, or go to work to bring in enough money. With that done, she could take time to enjoy lunch out or whatever small pleasures would get her mind off the ongoing problems.

How different it would have been to have a husband who would have hugged her when she walked in the door from work and said how nice she looked and what a good job she had done. Instead she got constant criticism from Dan. That was a sickness of his; he had to put his wife down to build his ego up. I guess he didn't think too much of himself, although he thought he was too good to clean the house or to do laundry. He was the old chauvinist pig type who ordered his wife around and then stalked into bed. Now he is in for a rude awakening. The quiet, soft-spoken little blond woman is carrying a big stick now, and when she decides to act, the timing will be right.

What is a chauvinist pig? One who bullies his wife and shoves her around when she doesn't do every little command. He twists her arms and shoves her into walls. He throws temper tantrums, as well as food and furniture or whatever fits his fancy, and then stalks off to work or bed. He buries his head in the sand when a problem arises and lets his wife fight his battles and then accuses her of going all over a man if she so much as sits next to one in a booth in a restaurant. He deprives her of sex if she can't smile a hundred times a day. He expects the impossible. He fills his jacket sleeves full of wood putty before he takes up in his new residence in a different county. He unhooks electric wires so she can't turn on lights in the shop—that annoys him—as he tries to rest in his sick room with his television blasting to cut out the world. He puts freezer paper over his window for curtains; puts clothes on an old black buffet which he uses for a dresser; and collects the pieces of carpeting he scrounged up, remnants from building the new house which he is trying to deprive Mickey of now. Nice guy.

As an ex-mailman, retirement was supposed to be a time of enjoyment. No, the man went on to another woman; confessed at Christmas time; refused to join his family for the traditional Christmas Eve at Candy's house; and allowed his wife to bring home his gifts which he kept in his sick room for almost a year before he opened them. Sick? That's the understatement of the year.

The sad thing is that his instigators are taking him out to wine and dine him and to encourage him to give his wife the shaft. He doesn't need much help. His dirty old mind works constantly on what he will pull next: After six mean days, maybe one day he might not take his mean pill. He puts up a nice front. At work all they see is this happy smiling man, but when he hits home it is a different story. He stalks in, changes his clothes, and moves on to the next job. He has no time to visit or exchange a kiss; he's got to do little jobs for the old woman who pays men with her services. Mouth to mouth? Yuk, oral sex is a refined name for it.

She always calls on Friday nights because she is depressed. "Is my man there?" she asks. Mickey answers, "I don't know; is he yours? He certainly isn't mine." The nerve of the bitch. She came to the house with her little list one day and told Mickey all the things that needed doing at their place. She is observant; I'll say that much for her. When Dan walked in, she waddled out to greet him and smiled cunningly, "Dan dear, can you fix my little dear's car and porch swing?" When she can't drive her daughter brings her to Mickey's home so the two of them can play their little game; the daughter is taking up where the mother left off. She went out and shacked up after her husband died; her own husband was running with the town whore. Oh well, Dan got the dead husband's shoes.

I wonder if that is what they mean by filling another man's shoes? I don't think so. It means to crawl into the wife's bed while the husband isn't at home and then go home with a big smile on your face and treat your own wife like a piece of shit. He can call her dirty names, sneak around, and cheat because his wife didn't treat him right? What a cop-out. You know how men are. Not all of them are like that, just the bastards. They call themselves men, but it only takes one slut to corrupt their weak minds, and then they just can't help themselves. However if the wife goes over the fence, then she is labeled a whore!

The naive wife. She was stupid to trust that a man stayed home. She cooked him a nice strip steak on New Year's Eve while he napped. She woke him up when it was just right, served him, and then did the dishes! He burped, farted, and then went to bed to sleep, too tired to have sex as he only needed twenty hours of sleep. He told his wife that she didn't turn him on. He was a taker while his wife was a giver, and he would take everything she gave him and abuse her with his mouth the next day. Then he wondered why she wasn't romantic.

He called himself a man, I call it sick. When he didn't get his way he threw a tantrum. Nice guy? Creep! He threw how much he spent on her in his wife's face, took her for a fast ride, and then asked if he hurt her back. He said he'd take her to the doctor's tomorrow, because that would make his conscience feel better. He's all old alligator skin, cold-blooded, and ex-merchant marine. He was not a morning person, and he was not a night person; he complained about everything. You could count the pimples on his tongue as it hung out of his halitosis-filled mouth. The workaholic never had any money, but he moved on to another woman, told her lies, and she believed him.

The second woman should always talk to the first wife, then she deserves the bastard. Or should she find out for herself that he can pull the same tricks on her? Let her suffer with the old goat. She will always be number two; they get the leftovers from the first marriage. The man doesn't change; he gets number two in bed. That is the first wife's revenge. He won't last long because his prostate is wearing out from age. The second wife better not expect too much; he won't perform too long. His back is bad and his car is worn out.

The ex-mailman, he retired to drive his wife nuts. He yelled and screamed and then moved on to a new woman. He tried to make his wife fit his design, and when that didn't work, he ran and cried to his children or anybody that would listen to his tale of woe. He blamed his wife for everything in his life.

This was Dan. The next woman couldn't wait to get him; there was always a slut waiting for him. She thought she could change him; he'd show her. He'd call her a fucking bitch when she didn't perform to suit him. If she didn't like it she would hear his famous last words: "If you don't like it, there's the door." But the day you turned it around and told him, "there is the door," his eyes would bug out. How dare you speak to him like that with no respect; he was the King.

Mickey always wanted to serve him dogshit; he wouldn't have known the difference as he burped, farted, and left the table. Mickey always set a pretty table with homemade food made from scratch. She looked like a queen for him, but he gave her the shaft. "You're wearing your halo, Mickey." Famous last words from the loving husband. Slime Mouth was his nickname; you could have labeled him worse. What good would it do? You couldn't please him, so why try? He would yell until she got a headache. He went "blah, blah, blah" and then, so he didn't have to listen, he would walk out the door and go out and put up his front to his peers, so they would think he was a nice little guy. He was a sneaky little son of a bitch; like father like son. That is so true.

Dan called Mickey, mother; was he still searching for a mother? She is the mother of his children. He was a spoiled little boy; he didn't get disciplined when he was young. He treated his mother like a piece of shit as he did his wife. Then he reverted back to his second childhood, throwing his food and tantrums; that is sick. He thinks he is God's gift to women. He is heterosexual but he asked his wife to suck his tits; Jesus, he is one sick pervert.

That is what woman number two is waiting for. Should Mickey tell her? Naw! If she is dumb enough to listen to his lies, she deserves what she gets—that would be nothing, the leavings from the first marriage. He orders lobster while everyone else is content with a meager meal. The King expects the best, and to hell with the rest.

He is an expert at giving his daughters away at weddings; it is one of his better points. He can get his rocks off on his wife, but he can't take it. He bullies with a dirty mouth; that's good old Dan.

His wife still hears the echoes after a year; "Mickey! I've been wrong." Two days before Christmas, he couldn't have planned it better. He had divorce papers served on her sixty-second birthday; well, that was a first for a birthday present. He didn't believe in celebrating that date. Mickey always gave him a party. She made him a cake and made a big deal out of August 8, 1924. He was so nice he let her do all the work and the cleaning up so he could accept. He's good at that. It's one of his best traits. "We don't have anything in common," he'd say. Good old Dan; right you are. "You need another man!"

Dan was always such a quiet, nice little guy; not everybody thought so. The neighbors heard him share his voice for years. He bellowed like a bull; it echoed through the hills in his old home town. He saved all his meanness up for his wife. He liked to put the knife in and twist it when she was down; he threatened to break both of his wife's arms if she removed the whiskey from his house. He needed it as his crutch.

The last time he got his dirty mouth on his wife was the night she decided to take action. She called the sheriff and domestic violence and then he was crying to his wife that he was going to jail. He refused to take man-to-man counseling; now who do you think he can blame? It's about time he takes a good look in the mirror—that's what he expects the world to put up with. He is sick! He never apologizes and thinks he has never been wrong—Wow! Is he ever wrong!

Good old Dan, he quotes out of the Bible: Money is the root of all evil! The only times he ever enters church is for weddings, christenings, and funerals. Among his famous last words is, "The law protects the criminal." I hope the law doesn't allow this to be true. Will they? Mickey wonders. At first it seems that way, but we'll see when the next court date comes up.

Surviving Alone

This is how Mickey survived January 19, 1992 and the empty nest syndrome.

The Mother's Prayer: Fuck them all, when you get done fucking them—Fuck the other ten. Pray for the good and go to sleep.

When the kids were small Mickey knew how to be in touch with God. She simply asked Him to watch over them when they went out on dates or whatever. Mickey just rolled over and went to sleep; she was very tired from a hard day's work.

When Mickey tries to take over and do it her way, she gets knocked off her pedestal. She is one of those strong-willed, determined types. This sounds better than saying she always has to be right because letting go is rough. Mickey found this on a card quite a few years ago: "I'm doing what I should have done years ago, which is finding out who I am and what I want. I want to have a choice, and I want to make decisions through choice, not duty. It has to be better for me and for the people who love me and the people I love."

Mickey had saluted Dan with "Heil Hitler" many times—"Yes, Dan; no, Dan; right away, sir; fuck you, Dan." She would give him the finger behind his back. Mickey was sick of taking orders from the German husband. She didn't like being called "mother" by her husband. She earned the nicknames of Freddie and Silver Top Dumpy when she sat behind the coal stove trying to keep warm. Mickey was cold all her life like when we were living with snow drifts on the stairs. Those were the good old days. Mickey wore coffee bag curlers which were bent and twisted to give her kinky hair, or she would use a curling iron heated in the wood stove. Sister Virginia would often say when curling her hair, "Oh, did I burn your forehead?" Then we'd receive a slap on the side of the head from her.

Dan always told Mickey her halo was showing. Well she met "Sister Theresa" in Tony Roma's (the old Globe Hotel) one Sunday night. Dominick, a cute, handsome Italian also gave her his phone number. He wanted her to call him. He lived in Corning and was thirty years old. Mickey usually carried her Polaroid camera in the car. Damn, how she would have liked her picture with him. She told him she needed a handy man; he likes horses.

Mickey always did like the looks of Italian men with their thin little mustaches and dark wavy hair. She loved the smell of fresh sweat on a man—not stale sweat but fresh sweat. It was a sign of a hard day's work; who cared if he took a shower? When that man walked in the door at night, Mickey wanted to be his queen. She loved to dance to "It Was (Fascination)." She wanted to slow dance with a man's arms around her and to hell with a cold shower. "Help me make it through the night—Take the ribbons from my hair—Shake it loose and let it fall—All I'm asking is for your time—Help me make it through the night—Let the devil take tomorrow, but tonight I need a (man)."

Mickey began working in a new craft shop. In six hours she only had two customers, so she put together a display of wood crafts and learned all the store's procedures. She slept in a trailer at the new Arcade because a snow storm came in around three in the morning and she wanted to be sure she could make it for her first day on the job. She'd be back at work again on Saturday. That's all for that month; she didn't expect big sales for the month of February. Everyone was still broke from Christmas. Recession is just a new word for depression.

That night Mickey was back at the new house on Merlau Road. It was a little late, but she played her electric organ and called Alabama. Tommy was going to try to join the Navy. Every time Mickey played "Auld Lang Syne" to the special people over the phone, they couldn't believe it was her. Mickey was so proud of herself she had to share it. She talked to Ronda; was she getting Mickey some makeup at a good discount. Mickey also talked to Joyce and Marge and played the organ for all of them. It's her way of touching each of the people who were important in her life right then.

Dear Lee:

Cold, Brrr. There's not much snow, and it's only 9 degrees above zero. Last night it was 20 below in Arcade. We've had slick roads. My old '77 Cadillac with studded tires and a bag of sand in the trunk made the trip. I got new glasses with red rims on top last week; they're neat looking. "Old Festus" was real glad to see me when I got home. He survived in his dog house but loves the back entrance. We have heat out there now. I have paneled and papered two walls, and I have two more and the ceiling to do. The windows and door need painting.

I have ripped out Dan's sick room in the garage. It is now back to a two-car garage and is all insulated. I've done some myself, and some was done by two boys I hired to help at $2.00 an hour. However you know how kids are; they usually don't show up when you need them.

I had the Seville towed to the garage; it needed a catalytic converter put on. I am also having them check it out for other problems. It's got no guts and drags its ass, but I may decide to drive it again, who knows?

Dan is going to Wales Court again tomorrow night. I do not know for what; I do not have to go, but I'm still trying to find out for what. I talked to the assistant district attorney on Monday. He is supposed to be representing me. He doesn't think we have enough evidence for court. That's a real positive outlook. I say that with sarcasm; if I had enough payrolls to slip under the table, his case would probably be stronger. I'll call him again tomorrow.

It's 11:20 P.M. I've got my red fleece pajamas on and I'm going to crawl on the couch and unwind. It has been a long day; I've been up since 5:15 A.M.

My back is rotten; it hurts like hell. It is arthritis and scoliosis. My left leg is numb; damn the aging process. Dan tells me I've worked too hard. Probably from lifting cases of milk. Who knows?

Love, Mickey

Letter to Dan's lawyer—it was never sent to him, though.

November 4, 1992

I'm going to take the time to write this letter and enclose this issue from the Sunday paper so you will know the man you are defending in court. Also enclosed is the letter I received from him that next day.

It is almost a year since I received the first divorce papers. They were delivered on my sixty-second birthday, the day before I flew to the Cleveland Clinic to see Dr. Gorham. I left the ticket open as I did not know what the outcome would be. Because my name was not fed into the computer I was not allowed to be an "in-patient." I called Dr. Rebella from the clinic. His office called the Cleveland clinic and told me someone at the desk was lying. I was told by Dr. Capicotta and Dr. Rebella to try to see if they could rectify the bad surgery done in Sister's Hospital. No luck!

In June of 1991, I had a mammogram done which showed a lump in my right breast. I was to have a needle biopsy done. The doctor decided to remove the lump without me knowing. In August 1992, I was on my way to physical therapy for the bad back when my vehicle was hit in the back at a stop sign, causing still more back problems. This stress is caused from physical pain.

I have an answering machine in the house to take some of the stress off me. I call it my secretary. When I played it back one day there was a message on it with you and Dan; he didn't know it records all conversations. I had that plus more cassettes in family court with me to show Judge Flaughtery.

The district attorney I talked with was named Robert Schollof. I also spoke to District Attorney Spileto. He informed me that I did not have to appear in court in Holland Court. I spoke with a lady named Hocket on that day of court. I had the flu, but I said I would try to make it. As you know I got there too late. Did you advise Dan to plead not guilty? I think I know the answer to that question.

Your client committed perjury in family court. I have asked for the transcript from court. The first court order was from Judge Orberg with constable Frank Sawyer present. Dan told Mr. Sawyer, "See how she lives? Just like a pig." When we were living together, Dan called me a "fucking bitch" while I was on the phone talking to my sister in California whose husband had a severe stroke; two days later my sister had one. I called her at 11:00 P.M. because of the three hour time difference, also because rates are cheaper then. She went through the earthquake in Santa Cruz. In addition one of her sons was critical from a motorcycle accident. When she came to visit in June of 1991, she came to our family reunion. This event stemmed from a nephew of mine who was killed about eight years ago by faulty farm machinery. Our family bonds together and helps each other when these things happen. My mother was seventy-four years old at the time. I thought I would lose her, too. I spent many hours with my family and Michael's parents and took food home to Dan at night. When I would get home, Dan would yell and scream, "I am going to put you in an institution." That's sick, not to help or comfort your wife when there is a tragedy. From that accident, when you see the farm program on television, that is in honor of Michael O'Connor, sixteen years old. He is buried in Holmes Hill.

Figment of Your Imagination—Adding Insult to Injury

Mickey was cooking butternut squash when they arrived. She turned it off and told the men she would leave with them and apologized to them. They said not to worry and that they had seen all kinds; Mickey left with them. She returned later to see if she had remembered to turn the stove off. Dan came up on the deck and tried to get to her. He wanted to talk to her, or so he said, but Mickey refused because he would only start screaming. He doesn't know how to talk. When she returned a week later, the squash was moldy. She noticed Dan had removed the hooks on the screen doors so she couldn't lock them. That was the only way she could keep him from getting her.

Mickey woke one morning to look out her window; she thought she was seeing things. Dan had taken something and smashed three sides of the gazebo out, including the lattice work and screens. She didn't know what he used. An iron rod lay there; it looked like that was his weapon. He had also taken the steps from the camper and threw them in the brook. God this man is sick! While living in his sick room in the garage, he started having his car washed and his shoes shined. He also bought the kind of razors that you can throw away. This was unusual behavior; usually it is a sign the man in shacking up. No, not old Dan. Would his children believe it?

Dan went against Mickey's restraining order. Mickey went out to the garage on a Sunday morning, the last morning Dan spent in his sick room. She got in her car and drove out, stopping at the mailbox to get the Sunday paper. Dan came rushing out of the garage. Mickey couldn't get her window up fast enough. Dan grabbed her arm and bent the key in the ignition so badly it took Mickey some time to straighten it. By then she had locked the car door. She drove to the nearest pay phone and dialed 911. A truck left its motor running, so as the sheriff kept asking her questions, she couldn't hear him very well. The town had not given her the restraining order; they had procrastinated, and she needed the assistance.

January 1992

Mickey carried a can of fly spray with her for two months. She had been advised to spray Dan in the face if he tried to become violent with her. She had been making cassette tapes of his bizarre behavior for six years, otherwise no one would have believed her. The children thought it was all her doing. They hadn't been around to see how this man, whom they called father, acted.

When her mother was dying of brain cancer, he accused her of allowing her car to run out of oil. He filled it to the fullest, and she had it checked at a garage the next day. The attendant told her that it wasn't good for the car to have too much oil in it, and so he removed some.

She had been going to a chiropractor for three years, trying to keep on her feet so that she could work at the gift shop. Dan expected her to put wood in the wood furnace two or three times a day, even with a bad back; he never cared that it threw her back out as long as he came home to a warm house. He thought a woman should stay home twenty-four hours a day. She was allowed no pleasure. He would show up when supper was ready but in his own time. Then he would eat and crawl on the couch. He worked all day and thought that his wife didn't do anything. He thought he owned the couch; he also thought he was the King! That was his castle! He was too good to do dishes; that was below him. His thanks for having the meal waiting was a burp and a few farts before crawling to the boob tube. He had had his day. He was too tired to have sex. He had a headache.

The post office work was so strenuous; was he a workaholic? Dan complained to his wife for five hours about it one day as if he thought Mickey should go straighten out his problems. Boy, he would go in and tell them a thing or two! Bullshit! He only had a loud mouth when he was screaming at his wife. What a nice guy. It got to the point where she couldn't wait for him to recline and start snoring with his breath smelling like a day-old pipe; he hadn't brushed his teeth in a week. He just laid on the couch in his undershorts, exposing his privates—a real sex symbol! He would take a bath promptly at 10:30 every Sunday night. He started to improve along the way; he started wearing deodorant. Was it because someone finally told him, or was that when the girlfriend came into the picture?

Trusting little Mickey, she wondered and thought no, not her husband. She was a fool! Whenever men make a change, you can bet it is not for the wife; they are starting to try to impress someone else instead. All Mickey heard about is Paula. She's an old woman, divorced. Dan used to change his clothes there in between jobs; she gave blowjobs. Mickey wondered if that was why Dan would run at her beck and call? She would call the house when she got depressed, usually on a Friday night when Mickey was taking Dan out for fish. He never had any money, or so he said. Dan let his wife carry the purse; she was supposed to foot the bill because he worked all week, as if his wife didn't do anything. He would even let her drive him since he drove all week. He wanted to relax, so then he could bitch about the way she drove. Hail Hitler! A German man—nice guy.

Paula used to call the house when Dan wasn't home. "Is my man there?" "No, Paula. Is he your man? He sure as hell isn't mine," Mickey would reply. And he accused her of chasing other men! Well, that's how he gets his rocks off!

Hurry up; eat faster, because this poor man had a hard day. He had to get home so he could get his nap on the couch and then head off to bed. He had had his day. He got pissed if his wife went into the kitchen to work on crafts; she was supposed to sit in the living room and count the pimples on his stinking old tongue while he rested to get prepared for eight more hours of sleep. He couldn't understand why his wife couldn't be happy with this style. Saturday was his night of rest unless Mickey made plans. He was not the social butterfly! Sunday was his day to relax and read the Sunday paper, the death notices. Was he looking for his own or his wife's? He had a full day of mowing lawns; napping; eating; and oh yes, it's Sunday, so it's time to take that weekly bath. He had to put up that good front at the post office. They thought he was such a nice guy, old happy Dan. They should have asked his wife. The miserable bastard walked in the door and bitched about whatever he could, changed his shoes, and headed off to see Paula. She needed something, but his wife got shit!

Four children came from this marriage. Mickey tries to understand why the oldest one calls her an egotistical bitch. The second daughter labels Mickey a mean old bitch; a grandson passed that information to her while staying with his Grandma Mickey during a Thanksgiving break from college while he told her how he could hear his mother and her boyfriend having sex in the bedroom until he couldn't stand to listen. He would go some place so he didn't have to listen. What about the youngest daughter, Candy? She calls her Mother, but while this is going on, she tells her she isn't coming to her funeral.

This was said while Mickey was sleeping with her shoes on, not daring to get undressed, staying locked in the bedroom with her car keys in hand and her window open; she stayed ready to jump out and run if old Dan dared to come after her. She would pull the car in at the farthest end of the premises, sneak into the side door, and set the alarm for six o'clock so she could be gone before Dan got up. He was in his quarters in the sick room in the garage. He was holed up there with his door locked; he had his TV, paper, curtains, and scraps of rugs. Mickey took him some sheets one day when she felt sorry for him. That was after he tried to rip the plates off the camper because he wasn't going to let her drive it. It was in his name; he owned everything.

Mickey slept in campgrounds for most of the summer of 1992, not daring to go home. She would go to the house in the daytime and be gone before Dan got home. He had probably spent the day with his slut. No, for some of the day he worked so he could pay his lawyer and sneak in the divorce. He wanted to make his slut legal. Mickey decided to have an alarm system put on the house so she could start sleeping there and Dan couldn't harm her, so she contacted a security alarm company and had them come out to the house while Dan was a work or wherever he was. She made an appointment for the alarm to be installed. The day the men came to install it, Dan came out of the garage, yelling and telling them to get away from his house. He accused Mickey of taking knives after him. The men pretended they were going to use the phone and called the town clerk at the town hall to get a restraining order as the sheriff said they couldn't do anything unless they had it in their hands.

The police had already been to Dan's home, and he accused Mickey of stealing his gun. She had removed it the night before from his sick room while he was in the bathroom in the shop and hid it until he left, saying he was going to do his laundry. That was after he had gone to eat. She took the shotgun and hid it under the daybed in the house. The sheriff, who started yelling at her, asked her why she stole her husband's gun. She told him she thought she did his job, so he started yelling at her, "Don't get smart with me, young lady." The deputy town clerk took him inside the town building. I don't know what she said to him, but he changed his attitude when he came back out. They proceeded to 5501 Merlau Road where the incident had occurred. Dan gave them his new address; he said he was moving there that day. He had been making his plans for quite some time as he already had an unlisted number.

When Mickey got to the motel that night, the lady at the motel told her both her front tires were very low on air. Dan must have decided he would see that she didn't get too far with the car. It's a wonder she made it to the phone. Mickey had been trying to get sympathy for the trial to back up her story. No one wanted to get involved. She didn't blame them, but she needed them to at least make a written statement to corroborate her story. She needed proof!

The first night she finally called the sheriff in; he was afraid of the dog. How then would he protect her? He wore the gun, but would he be capable of protecting her when he was afraid of the dog? He thought it was just a domestic fight. He asked Mickey why she didn't just leave; she had decided not to run anymore. Enough is enough! In her heart she knew Dan needed help. The sheriff finally asked Dan why he didn't leave. He claimed not to have heard; he had his back turned at the time, and he does have a hearing problem. Then he ran around telling people Mickey threw him out. He always told Mickey, "If you don't like it here, there is the door." He thought he owned the house and his wife had no rights—wrong!

Mickey had asked him for the keys to the house so she could sleep without him coming in the middle of the night. He lied; he was still entering. So one day she broke through the insulation in his sick room and took his clothes. They were so dirty. She left him a note that she was going to wash them. However after she brought them to the house, she changed her mind and threw them in the closet. They were missing the next day. He had lied; he still had a key.

Deciding it was not safe to stay at the house anymore, she checked in at a campground. She asked not to be listed there so that she could get some rest and continue her craft work. She spent most of her time for the summer of 1992 at the campground, but with colder weather coming, she had to make other provisions. She decided to go to the house if she got the sheriff's protection. She couldn't keep running. She would draw the blinds to cover the windows and keep all the lights on outside but keep the inside dark; she watched a little TV. She even bought a different car so she would feel safer out in public. However it didn't take Dan long before he knew what she was driving.

Mickey went to the plaza and saw his station wagon parked there. She circled and parked a few cars away only to find out that Dan knew the car. She laid down on the front seat for quite some time. She took a cosmetic case, snapped off the mirror, and proceeded to watch what he might do. He sat for quite some time then laid rubber when leaving. I guess he will never learn. Mickey heard him say for forty-five years, "The law protects the criminal!" Wrong! He never thought he was ever wrong.

She knew he was there as she could hear him rapping his pipe on the outside of the door of the station wagon before he refilled it. She headed back to the campground. She had bungee straps on the doors so it was safe there with the night patrol cruising through on his three-wheeler. There she would rest well.

Candy's voice echoed in her ears, "The man wants a divorce!" Mickey knew that was not the answer. Dan was a very sick man; he was emotionally disturbed. This had been going on for quite some time. The bad thing, the wrong thing was that she tried to handle it all by herself. When she finally brought it to light, no one would believe her.

Dan had asked permission to come to the house to pick up his personal papers and tools. This was granted by the judge. With the constable present, Mickey went out to the garage to see what he was taking. He turned to the constable and said, "See how she lives? Just like a pig!" Mickey was disgusted all night; he even dumped her ashtray in the driveway. After Dan pulled out, she invited the constable in for coffee. It was quite evident that Mickey was anything but a pig. Her house was always very neat. Mickey always picked up as she didn't like clutter! With no children in the house, this was an easy job.

Just having old Festus lying in the back entrance of the house gave her the feeling of security. He only barked if someone was walking on the road or pulling into the driveway. She took him in so he wouldn't be put to sleep. It turned out to be the best decision she ever made. He was part husky and part black Labrador and would probably attack anyone trying to harm his mistress! A dog is man's best friend—also woman's! He is here for many reasons.

Mickey's Strength

Life is like an apple tree that keeps spinning around: Some of the apples are golden, some are rotten, some are juicy and sweet, and some are hard while some are soft. It is up to us as human beings to learn when to pluck the right ones at the right time. The golden ones are few and far between. There are more rotten ones, but we learn fast not to eat the rotten ones. Do we need the golden ones to give us happiness? It depends on what we need as individuals to make us happy.

Mickey never wanted to be a millionaire; she just needed the security of knowing she had not spent the electric bill money. Millionaires have many false friends; they are loved only for their money. Who needs them? No one who will not share his guts with you is a true, honest friend; they will not tell anyone. A true friend will love you through the bad times and the good times. They will accept you as you are and not try to change you. Hearts warm when good friends meet. It is a picture that has hung on Mickey's walls in many rooms. She just gives it another coat of paint to match whatever room it is moved to.

A favorite poem of Mickey's has brought her through many tough times. She found it in the newspaper many years ago:

God give me sympathy and give me strength,
To keep my courage high,
God give me health and happiness, and
Keep a twinkle in my eye.

I guess this is how she kept her sense of humor through the bad times. When a situation arises that is impossible and seems to have no answer, she bursts into laughter. When there is no rhyme or reason, she bursts into laughter.

She finally went back to high school to get her diploma at age fifty-seven, realizing that life had taught her the values it took to pass. The diploma is a piece of paper that society says you need to get a job in the nineties. She had progressed from a little girl who was scared to death to make a book report in English class about Old Ichabod Crane. The school tried to change her. She loved dogs and horses; she loved all the animals. She ran through the cow feces or Heifer dust because the farmers had healthy feet; she knew a little "101" would wash it off and get rid of the smell. She always wanted to become a housewife, a mother who baked homemade bread and yeast doughnuts as well as cookies which she made in a wood oven.

Now at sixty-two she is highly educated, but now nobody wants to listen to her wisdom. Damn, that is frustrating. Oh well, such is life!

Hard Times

After Dan became violent, Mickey carried a can of fly spray with her whenever she went down to talk to him in the garage where he had his sick room. He kept it locked, but all he had for walls was insulation, so she could rip it down and enter when she wanted to look around and see if he was up to something.

Mickey made cassette tapes of their conversations six years ago and many more that past summer. No one would have believed her if she hadn't done so.

They were having a conversation one night in April of 1991, and he sat and threw about a pound of M&M candies at Mickey one by one as she sat on the couch. She just sat there and laughed at him and told him she felt sorry for him. She refused to pick them up. Mickey told him that Jody, the girl who she had clean the house, would want to know what they were doing there, so he picked them up. Another time Mickey had asked him to pick up some orange roughy at the grocery store. She was talking to him as he was ready to go outside. He whipped around, grabbed the fish out of the refrigerator, and threw it at her. It splattered all over the couch and up the wall. He started yelling. "That's all you care about is your damn couch."

Mickey felt sorry for him but didn't know what to do. She wouldn't even dare to ask the kids for help, as they treated her like she was not supposed to have any brains. Her oldest daughter called her an egotistical bitch; her second daughter was not so bad until Dan went to her the day they had a real row about signing the mortgage for the house.

Cap was there from California and was staying with Mickey so she could go to the family reunion. Our other two sisters were there visiting her. Mickey had some concrete statues to paint outside. Every time she went outside to work on them, Dan would come out of the garage from his sick room and start screaming at her. He wanted to know if she was going to sign the papers closing the mortgage on the house they had built in the fall of 1990. Mickey told him she would but that she really didn't want to sign anything with him anymore because he was acting so nutty. She went into the house several times so he would leave her alone. She would wait a few minutes and then go out the side door, thinking he would probably leave for work. She locked the door each time she went in so he wouldn't be able to follow her in.

Mickey finally just gave up and decided to stay in and have a cup of coffee with the girls. He knocked on the door and wanted to know if "Mother" was in there. Mother, of course, was Mickey. She opened the door, and he came charging in and started screaming at Cap. He told her that she better tell her goddamned sister to straighten out or she would be sorry. Mickey started moving toward him, telling him to get out of the house and leave them alone. Mickey told him she fully intended to sign the damn mortgage, but he just kept screaming. She kept talking and backing him toward the door, and when she finally got him outside, Mickey told him to shut up. He wouldn't, so she reached down and picked up a pail half full of water and threw it in his face. He started moving toward her, and I'm sure he intended to hit her. When he got really close, Mickey grabbed him on both sides of his face, raking her fingernails down both cheeks. That really infuriated him, and he took off in the station wagon. He came back about a half hour later with a harassment order he had a sheriff write up on her and told her he was going to have her locked up. Everyone cleared out. Mickey went to physical therapy, and the girls went to our brother Dan's house. Mickey called her husband from East Aurora and told him she would meet him at the bank at 5:45 P.M.

Mickey was terrified to go to the bank, not knowing what he would pull there. She stayed at a friend's house until it was time to meet him. While she was there she called another girlfriend and asked her to meet her when she came out of the bank for moral support. Mickey could have kissed her. They got in her car and went down a side street where Mickey dissolved into tears. She went to a motel that night so that she could get some rest. She had been tying the door shut with an extension card and propping chairs under the door knobs so he couldn't go charging in on her in the middle of the night.

His temper tantrums had been coming more often by then. He just wasn't rational. Mickey figured she knew how to cure a child when they threw a tantrum; you just let them keep banging their head until it hurts. But this one was beyond her. Old men go to jail, and they can beat bars. Was this a second childhood? Who knows. Anyhow he had a brush cut, so they wouldn't have to cut his hair when he got there.

One time when he came out of his sick room, he hacked up a mouthful of saliva and spit it at Mickey. Our sister works at Attica prison. She told Mickey that's what the prisoners do to the guards as they walk by. She didn't know what he would do next.

The Struggle Continues

Mickey went to work at the Sio Gift Shop in 1985. She went to a garage sale with our sister, Virginia. Using money from the first paycheck, she bought a black and white TV for ten dollars for the garage which they used as a recreation room in the summertime. Dan asked her if she intended to move upstairs into the empty apartment they had. Mickey said, "Why don't you?"

Mickey did move up there for five weeks. She was going to adult education classes for her high school diploma, working five days a week, and attending physical therapy for three nights a week after work. She had to move back downstairs because her back wouldn't take carrying groceries and other things upstairs. Mickey put a slide bolt on the stair door so Dan couldn't come up during the night. She ordered oil for the furnace, but when she tried to go downstairs to get her checkbook to pay for it, she found that Dan had put locks on all doors so she couldn't get in.

Mickey invited Todd Wilson, one of her grandchildren, to spend the night. Dan came in from the garage and backed her up against the kitchen sink; he wanted to know where she had spent all of his mother's money from the inheritance. He had taken two thousand dollars to pay his delinquent bills, and Mickey had put a thousand into an IRA account. He wanted her to account for every cent. She asked him not to act like that with Todd in the house, and she offered to take Todd home after Dan left to go to work. Todd said he wanted to stay with her, so they went upstairs that night to sleep. Mickey locked the door so Dan couldn't come up; she didn't want Todd upset by his grandfather's actions. She took him home the next morning so she could go to work that next day.

The following year, our mother was dying of brain cancer. Mickey had all the Christmas breads and candies on the shelf for Christmas Eve for our family. She had told us all that we wouldn't have Christmas Eve together if he was too bad. Dan came in from the garage and accused her of running her car out of oil. He threw all the Christmas baked goods on the kitchen floor and told her to go to her friends at church. He resented her going to church on Sunday. He said he would go with her, but it was too far to drive; it's only on Southwestern in Orchard Park. It was Mickey's way of going someplace on Sunday. She would browse in K-Mart and maybe go out to lunch with the ladies from the church.

Dan told Mickey our mother said she never loved her that day. That wasn't true. She died three days later. I don't know why he even went to the funeral with Mickey. He made fun of her all their married life. Mickey asked him to go the day of the funeral but told him it really didn't matter to her. He had always made nasty remarks about our family. I guess he thought he was better than we are, but you'd have to ask him why? He did the same to her in public. That was the only way he could make himself look good. He would tell their personal life to friends when she was with him—about their problems with sex in marriage—anything to embarrass her. He told a brother-in-law that she wouldn't put wood in the wood furnace. That was when she was going to a chiropractor three days a week just so she could work at the gift shop. Mickey had thrown her back out trying to lift chunks of wood when leaving for bowling one day; he told her that was her problem.

Dan accused her constantly of having relationships with other men even if she just talked to them. Our sister Virginia was beaten by her husband after one of her children's weddings because Dan kept feeling her up at the wedding. He got drunk that night; I guess that eased his conscience. A couple of months ago, Dan told Mickey that he talked to her about it. That's not true; Mickey asked her. He told Mickey that he was going to have her put in a mental institution if she couldn't put up with his behavior. Mickey had a nervous breakdown years ago because he was playing around with her best girlfriend. Ever since then she wouldn't do everything to suit him; then he threatened her that he would have her put away.

Mickey's daughters do the same. Whatever he tells them, they believe. I don't know what he has been running to them or his friends with now. Anyhow, the letters she gets from her daughters—and their phone calls—are bad enough. She doesn't even want to read them. They never put anything in the past; Dan doesn't either.

Mickey had been going through menopause ever since she had to have a hysterectomy about ten years ago. Mickey and Dan went to Rev. Gicheringer for counseling. He told Dan she needed to be treated with kindness and love. As you can see by the evidence she brought to court, these are the results. Dan told her he was going out and shacking up. He jumped up and down on the flowers she had planted that spring. She had been asked to be tested—for her own protection—for venereal diseases because he wouldn't say how safe he had been. Mickey had never cheated on the marriage. If he had, I think he should be the one to be tested. I saw no reason why Mickey should be the one to pay for a test when only Dan could tell you if it was needed. Ask him and the one he'd been with. Then we would all know if it was necessary. I thought it was a disgrace to Mickey and to his children and grandchildren that she had to be put in that situation.

I don't think much of a woman who goes out with a married man anyhow. They will only hear how bad they were treated at home. Dan had no reason to go outside of their marriage for his needs; he made the choice.

He told Mickey she was only threatening to do something. He was wrong. I just hope he was wrong for all the years he said the law protects the criminal. He committed a misdemeanor; the law says he would serve up to five months in jail and that counseling was mandatory. Mickey was told he would get psychiatric help once he was in jail. She prayed to God that the law was on her side. She did not want any more verbal or physical abuse. Dan wanted her to drop the case and told her things would get better. She knew better! If she couldn't be perfect every day and do what he said—she worked like a dog—he would take her for a fast ride in the car. He threatened her this way for years. If she didn't like it, there was the door.

In 1947 he had a bad car accident in the first year of their marriage. He rolled the car over four times. For awhile after that, Mickey told Dan that it made her nervous if he drove fast. Then he took her for a fast ride at 80 miles per hour and told her he would show her how to get nervous.

They went to visit the Lindhomes years ago where he just sat and drank and told them one lie after the other about Mickey. He threatened to run her into a telephone pole and kill her. She begged him to take her home to her children. It was Mickey's best girlfriend that he wanted, he was always in the back seat of a car with her at every party. Then he would want to know why Mickey was upset the next day.

For any vacation they ever had Mickey did all the work getting ready for it. He would throw in her face how much money vacations cost. If she got upset and cried, then she spoiled the whole vacation. Dan never planned a vacation; he pouted on every one they took and expected everyone to wait on him while he was there; after all it was his vacation, why should he do anything? About eight years ago Mickey told him, "If you don't like it, there's the door." He replied that no wife of his would ever say that and get away with it.

Mickey always had a good meal waiting for Dan when he got home. Often he would choose to drink and not come home, and then he would complain if the meal was cold even at eight o'clock at night when she originally had it ready between five thirty and six o'clock. The house couldn't be too clean for him. She kept it picked up and vacuumed once a week. She also did laundry once a week. Because she put his clean clothes on the bed one time, Dan didn't talk to her for five days when she went to work at the gift shop because she put his clean clothes on the bed. Mickey couldn't bend down and put them in the drawers—her back wouldn't allow it. He called her a fucking bitch when she wouldn't do what he thought she ought to do.

About a year earlier he asked Mickey to sign a loan with him to build a new house. She should have known better. When she went to the bank to get it changed to a regular mortgage, she was embarrassed to take the papers in. There were coffee stains all over them. She couldn't discuss anything with him; he threw food at the walls, and she refused to clean up after him. Three days after she signed for the mortgage he wanted a divorce.

Everyone kept trying to talk her out of having him put in jail. She wanted him there so she could get some rest. He had threatened to have all the utilities at the house shut off, which didn't make much sense to her. The pipes would all freeze in winter. He had already taken his name off the gas utility. They called Mickey to see what was going on.

This behavior did not start when he retired, like everyone thinks. Another example of his strange behavior was the time he got involved with some companies that got orders over the phone when he was still working. He ordered two hundred dollars worth of hand cleaners and then wanted Mickey to refuse it when it came; he also ordered over one hundred dollars of some product to dump in his gas tank. These people were calling Mickey at various times of the day, sometimes even at six-thirty in the morning. She told Dan she was going to have their phone number changed and unlisted if he didn't stop.

Mickey thought perhaps his work load was too heavy so she tried to get him to stop taking on more work than he could handle. He ripped the phone off the wall and smashed it. This was when she had back surgery. Dan kept screaming that they had no money. Mickey was going to clean out the camper and unplug it to save on electricity. He was furious as he was using it to cook and refrigerate in. He started to take the plates off of it that night so she couldn't drive it anymore. She taped his ranting that night. Mickey left most nights never knowing what he would try next. She got up one morning and looked out the window; he had smashed two sides of the gazebo out. He said he had built it himself, which was not true. Mickey had helped him with it.

He had not given Mickey any money with which to live from October until the middle of November. She confronted him in a restaurant, and then he mailed her some. The Sunday he moved out of the garage and into his apartment he accused her of stealing his gun from the room in the garage. He had the gun and a box of new shells standing in the corner. He hadn't used the gun in years and told the sheriff that it didn't work. Mickey asked them to check it as he lies so much that she couldn't believe him. The didn't check it, and he took it with him when he moved. He threatened to blow her head off that day, so she went to a motel that night. The air was very low in both front tires of the car the next morning; the car had been in the garage by his room that night.

Mickey went to the bank to get a mortgage started on the house. They had a temporary loan to build it. Dan asked her to sign for it when they started to build, but it was draining them financially. Three days after she signed for the mortgage, he told her he wanted a divorce.

He tried to tell Mickey and everyone else that she threw him out of the house. He said he didn't hear Sheriff Basnnan suggest that he leave in June. Mickey can't talk to him about anything without him screaming and throwing things; it was the same way when they lived in the trailer.

Mickey's main purpose in following through on the court order was to see that he would be put in jail so that he could be seen by a psychiatrist. He admitted having depression one time when Mickey asked him what was wrong with him. He told her he was ready to quit this any time she wanted to, but getting a divorce wasn't going to solve their problems. Mickey has asked her lawyer for a legal separation. Dan kept having divorce papers served on her even after he sat in her lawyer's office and said he wanted to separate for a year. Mickey said six months had been suggested. Judge Norberg gave him permission to come to the residence to pick up one of his table saws. Mickey walked out when he was ready to leave with the constable present. She was disgusted one night when she drove into the yard and saw that he had dumped her car ashtray in the driveway. He told the constable, "See how she lives? Just like a pig. Oink. Oink."

He accused her of being out with a man last year when she went to a craft show with her daughter-in-law and also of being all over one of the men in a restaurant in Strykersville because she sat in a booth talking with a young man. Mickey and Dan had met him at a Halloween party a couple of years earlier. She told him he looked so much like her son she could just hug him and kiss him on the cheek.

Mickey lived in the camper for six weeks that fall. She didn't dare go home except in the daytime when he was at work. She would leave before he got home or in the early evening. She carried a can of fly spray with her for the last two months Dan was living in the garage. He lived in a room in the garage for about two weeks after the protection order was issued. Mickey went down to his room to give him a phone message from one of his carpenter customers on Friday night, September 27. He had been out for a couple of hours, and she asked him where he had been. He said he had been out to do his laundry. Mickey had a few words with him and asked him if there was another woman involved. He wouldn't look her in the eye but stood looking at the corner of the garage, then he bragged about having sex with her for eight or nine months.

Mickey went out to the mailbox on September 29 to get the Sunday paper. She drove her car out of the garage (she usually keeps all the car doors locked) and put the window of the driver's side down to reach in the mailbox for the paper. Dan came out of the garage, walking fast, and grabbed the key to the car and bent it almost in half, scratching her hand while doing it. She got the window up, straightened the key so that she could drive to a phone booth in South Wales, and called the sheriff's office. O'Brien and Gorlach met her in Wales Center where she had gone to pick up the protection order as she had not received it yet. Gorlach and O'Brien started yelling at her and wanted to know why she stole Dan's shotgun. She had removed it the night before from his room and took it in the house and put it under a couch. When he went to the back of the shop, he also threw some of the shells out into the yard—some of them were still laying out there. He told the sheriff it didn't work, but they didn't even check it. He had a box of new shells with it, but he hadn't shot that gun in about five years. He probably wouldn't have even thought about it, but O'Brien came back to the door when she called him in June and wanted to know if we had any guns on the premises. Mickey laughed and said up in the loft of the garage. Mickey hadn't shot a gun since she was thirteen years old. She didn't even like having them around because children could get them and get hurt. She wanted to know why Dan wasn't arrested that Sunday in September. He had violated the protective order. He had been told in court to stay away from Mickey. After the protection order was issued, Dan still went on the property and took things out of the shop, such as work supplies. Jack Lowe, a retired electrician who Dan knew, was there one day. Mickey doesn't know if he helped Dan mess up the electric wires in the switches for the shop or not, but when she returned a couple of days later, the lights in the shop wouldn't work and all the light bulbs were removed from the back of the shop and upstairs in the loft of the garage. Mickey called George Hawley to fix them. He signed a paper before he fixed them, explaining what had been done to them and told Mickey that Dan had stopped him while working at Elizabeth Hochwarter's and admitted what he had done.

House of Spite

Mickey was going to have Shield Security Systems put a security system on the house on 10 September 1992, so she could come back and live in the house. She thought it would be wise if she wanted to go out. Dan usually went to work every day, but that day he was still home when the men came to install it. He came out of the garage, his sick room, and started yelling at them when they wanted to check the doors going into the cellar. Mickey told them just to ignore him as he had been acting strange lately. One man came in the house and made believe he was using the phone. He said not to worry about it and that they had a phone in the truck. They would just cancel it. Mickey hasn't had it installed yet as Dan won't send the money unless he feels like it.

Dan had his name taken off the Burnwell Gas Company bill. He thought Mickey should pay for gas to heat the house, but his name was on the mortgage, and if Mickey didn't watch over the house pipes they would freeze when the gas ran out. The same is true with the shop. Dan said he had no money—wrong! He paid for an apartment in Cowlesvile. He threatened to have the phone at 5501 Merlau Road shut off if she didn't pay the bill.

Mickey flew to the Cleveland Clinic on November 6. Dr. Capicotta and Dr. Ruben both told her to go there to see if she could get help for her back problem, which she had had for the last five years; both legs would go numb and the pain was excruciating. Mickey had the surgery done three years earlier. The surgery didn't help. The same problems remained. Dr. Capicotta confirmed she had arthritis in the discs. They pinched off the L-4 nerve which caused the pain and numbness in both legs. She also had arthritis in her neck.

Mickey's car was hit in the rear end at a stop sign on her way to physical therapy. Both legs and arms went numb as a result of the accident. She is still going to Ed Koch two times a week for physical therapy. She has back spasms all the time which are very painful and takes Darvon when the pain is excruciating. That allows her to keep going.

Mickey was referred to the pain clinic at General Hospital on Bailey Avenue by Dr. Goren at the Cleveland Clinic. She is waiting for them to set up an appointment and plans to try to get the senior citizen's bus to transport her there. She is not able to work outside of the home and cannot collect disability. The Darvon creates some side effects, so she won't take it unless it is absolutely necessary.

She had an appointment to have a picture taken at Eames Store. Mickey thought she would try to get a job doing television commercials, something that wouldn't be so strenuous on her back. The picture she had taken showed the black and blue marks on her right arm from Dan twisting it the night he shoved her into the door and told her she was a crazy old bitch who had a sloppy cunt, baggy tits, and an ugly face. That was in April 1991. She had to have a lump removed from her breast that spring. Dr. Godfrey did the surgery at Mercy Hospital. Thank God it wasn't malignant. Dan told Mickey he didn't give a damn if it was. He called himself a bastard—it's probably the first truthful thing he said in the past six months.

He lied about having a phone in his room in the garage. Mickey tried to call Mr. O'Malley one day at four o'clock. The phone in the house wasn't working. She went down to the garage and asked him if he was messing with the phone down there; he indicated he wasn't. That night Jock Lowe came out to see Dan about working at his new house. Mickey went down to the garage to tell Jock she was not taking work calls for Dan as it was too painful to get up and answer phone calls sometimes. Dan made a dirty remark to her and said Jock knew how she was. Mickey had always been nice to Jock Lowe when he went to their house. If he knew anything different, it was only what Dan had told him about her.

Dan told her Jock Lowe told him he hung up on her a few nights earlier when he called the house; he lied. Our sister from California was visiting Mickey's house. She had driven her to Springville to see her friend in a nursing home, but while going home, both legs went numb while she was driving. Mickey was lying on the couch with ice packs on her back. The phone rang; she was going to let it go on the answering machine, but Capitola, our sister, said it might be one of her kids calling. She had had a stroke, and they called often to see how she was doing.

Mickey said she would answer it. It was Jock Lowe calling wanting to know if Dan was there. Mickey talked with him briefly and told him she wasn't going to answer the phone but she had changed her mind. Maybe that's why Dan and Jock were such good friends.

Mickey thought it was nice that his friends could come and have a beer in the shop together. Dan had prostate problems, and the doctor told him to stay away from beer and coffee. The only reason she would suggest he not drink beer was that he wet his pants in the car when they were in California three years ago, but since the doctor told him not to, he drinks it all the time. That didn't make sense to Mickey but that was up to him.

Jock and Dan went to The Moose one night. Mickey asked Dan something about a craft she was working on. He started throwing the wooden foot stool, the piano accordion, and various other things across the living room. I don't know why he was throwing a temper tantrum. It took no reason at all then. No one had better cross him; Mickey knew that. He told her he had depression. I don't know why; you'd have to ask him. Mickey was not going to allow him to cripple her with his moods. She knew he needed help, but he refused to get it. She offered to make an appointment at a psychiatrist for him, but he refused.

He told her he was going to rip the plates off the camper one night so she couldn't drive it. Mickey took it to Three Valleys which is about fifteen minutes from her home. They had a membership there. It was the only vacation she could get. Dan got furious one night at camp because he started a fire in a small grill under an awning. The smoke was getting in Mickey's eyes so she took a walk to the john. When she came back, he said he'd had enough. It was only the first or second night they were there, and he said he was going home. Everyone at camp wanted to know what was wrong with him. Mickey told them she didn't know and that she guessed he was just in a bad mood.

His behavior was getting worse. He told her that he had been wrong but wouldn't tell her what he had done. He told her she could have anything she wanted then sent her divorce papers. That did make sense to me.

Mickey was going to a craft show in Alden one day. Since Dan had his apartment, she had written him a letter. Mickey thought she'd stick it in his back door instead of mailing it. When Mickey called him to ask something on the phone a couple of nights later, he told her she was snooping. He must have had something to hide, but you'd have to ask him.

Mickey had a jacket of his which he had left at the house when he was packing some of his clothes. Guess what she found in the sleeves: caulking compound, I guess. He had filled both sleeves and let it harden.

At the cemetery on Vermont Hill Road in South Wales, New York, Mickey thinks of taking something bad and turning it into good. It is good to comfort people when they are hurting. That is the way Mickey was raised. It still upsets her to see parents allowing their kids to ride tractors, especially on the fenders of tractors. Parents are supposed to guide and protect their children. Mickey is the mother of four: three daughters and one son. She wanted every one of them until they were eighteen years old. If she couldn't get enough good teachings and standards in to them by then, she felt she had lost them anyhow. Mickey now has eleven grandchildren and one great-grandchild. She considers it a privilege. Mickey has touched each one of their lives. Mickey may not be God, and she is not perfect, but she is Mom and Gram. Mickey has some kids that are her proxy grandchildren. They are neighborhood kids that were friends of her children. One of her favorites—they are all her favorites, each special in his or her own way—goes to her to ask advice. "You never steer me wrong, Gram; you're my idol," one said. What a privilege. Another one asked, "Do you believe in God, Grandma?" Mickey replied, "Yes Katie, he made grandmas." All the time she is hoping she is giving them the answers they are searching for. Katie was a latchkey child. Fred was her dog and her friend.

Three days before our mother died of brain cancer, Dan threw all the Christmas cookies, candy, and preparations onto the kitchen floor. He accused Mickey of running her car out of oil (he had filled it too full of oil himself) and then told her her mother never loved her. Our mother was murdered in Mercy Hospital by an overdose of chemotherapy. Mickey was told his the night before she had her breast surgery last year. Our sister thought she should know. A nurse overdosed her but apologized for it.

Dan went into a depression after his mother died. He yelled at her and treated her terribly. She would cry to Mickey when she went to visit her. "Why doesn't Dan come to see me?" she would ask. Mickey would try to comfort her. "I don't know, Grandma, I don't know." She had a sick husband. He tried to make out with Mickey when her second daughter was three months old. When Grandma would go out to play cards, he came up the stairs with his whiskey bottle. He tried to seduce many women in Wales.

Last year, after they moved into the new house, Dan brought in his whiskey bottle, but he wasn't drunk. The image of his father passed before Mickey. He sat in his chair and started laughing like an idiot. "Look at you, you crazy old bitch, with your baggy tits, sloppy cunt, and ugly face." He twisted Mickey's wrists and then shoved her into the back door while trying to throw her out. Before that she was told, "If you don't like it, there's the door!" No man should be able to make his wife a cripple. Mickey is not a fucking bitch! Since he received the letter, he has called her a "fucking broad."

He came to 5501 Merlau Road and ripped open the window Mickey had nailed down because they were having three and four break-ins a week in Wales. The garage door was jammed, and he had battered it in. Dan had used a crowbar to rip open the garage windows. Mickey came home from East Aurora one afternoon and noticed someone had been inside the house because things had been taken from the property. She called Dan to ask him to make up a list of what he had removed. He refused.

Dan threatened her with a knife. Mickey sat there in court listening to them defending a man—a sick man, I think—trying to prove adultery. He has accused her of allowing many men to go all over her whenever she would sit next to another man. He has accused her of other rotten things, too. Mickey refers to liars as having a split tongue and backbiters as having a forked tongue. Dan had to put her down in public to make himself look good. He thought Mr. O'Malley was stupid! Mickey's method, when someone seemed to think they knew everything was to just keep quiet; eventually they would hang themselves. That is what Dan did in family court; the transcript was proof of it. If Dan had problems, he brought them all on himself. Why would you want this sick human being running free? To hurt another woman or some young girl?

Dan asked Mickey to suck his tits while they were married. Isn't that a sign of homosexuality? Everyone kept asking Mickey questions. The should have asked Dan what he did with his money. Dan told Mickey he was sick! She couldn't solve his problems; he had to solve them. "Do you like homosexuals?" I know there are gays—was Mickey living with one and didn't know it? In my opinion, I think homosexuals make a choice to become gay.

Mickey has children and grandchildren. "You are our leader!" they told her. She is leading; if they follow, it's up to them. How about the system? People run the system and a few get caught. They laugh, hire a lawyer, and try to buy themselves off. Everyone is entitled to a lawyer telling them to plead not guilty.

Mickey let her inspection on the car expire. She went to court, pleaded guilty, and was fined. Every case of drunk driving pleaded not guilty. Mickey knew everyone of them lied. Dan had become such a pro at lying he could no longer decipher the truth from reality.

Mickey went out to breakfast after church. Dan asked her if she was going out cuckholding. She called the sheriff the first time, he would stand in the shop and pretend that he was jerking off in the window. That is sick! Anyone with any intelligence would not keep him out in society acting like this. I'm sure you have to go to college to become a lawyer. I question if it's his intelligence, unless you aren't married and hate women and children. When Mickey sat in family court, she wondered how do you change the system? How do you change a sick society? What about parents who stand up for their children when they are wrong, don't discipline the child, and don't say no? Visit a prison—that's where they end up and learn even more dirty habits. They bring a criminal on a television show to show anyone with half a brain how to break every security system. Does that make sense to you? It doesn't to me.

Keep the drunk on the road until he kills someone. Innocent people die every day from someone else's mistakes. Should we ask a bartender to tell when someone is drunk? Anyone who has drank knows sometimes it only takes one or two drinks to reach the stage of not being able to drive; other times it takes five, six, seven, or eight drinks.

Dan came home from Lockport where he was supposed to be working, bragging that he had thirteen limes in his gin and tonic glass. But for the grace of God he hasn't killed someone yet. He thought Mickey should drive him home puking and falling on the floor with his pants around his knees. He couldn't even undress and go to bed; he fell in the driveway with his good clothes on and cut his head.

Mickey refuses to help a man who acts like that. She believes a person picks up the glass on his own and is responsible for himself. Only one made him do it. Dan has blamed her for every mistake he has made ever since they got married. She told him to look at the man in the mirror. When he sees what looks back at him, that is what he expected her to live with.

It was too bad he didn't accept help in Wales Court. Mickey was told by the sheriff that it was mandatory—wrong! Not to accept help is sick! Telling Mickey Dan is sick couldn't help him. She knew he was either physically or mentally sick eight years ago. Mickey felt the money his lawyer accepted from him would have been better spent paying bills or going on a vacation, something pleasant. What do you think?

"Do you have to tell everything, Mickey?" your client asked her. She would not sweep it under the carpet for him. Did he really think he could win in court that day? Common sense would tell me differently. Dan had wanted someone to feel sorry for him every day since she married him. The tape was from the answering machine with Dan and his lawyer talking. That's too bad, Dan.

The German Bastard, Dan

If you see this man, run like hell in the opposite direction. As long as you salute him (Heil Hitler) you can live in his domain. He likes to keep his wife sick and to manipulate and control her. If she doesn't perform to suit him, he will label her a fucking bitch. God, what a nightmare.

He smashed furniture and threw Easter-colored M&Ms in his wife's face one at a time; an entire pound of them. The only reason he picked them up was that Mickey told him the girl was coming to vacuum the next day and she would tell her how they got on the floor. He threw orange roughy at Mickey because she asked him a question as he was going out the door. It splattered all over the couch and up the wall. When Mickey started cleaning it up, he turned to say, "That's the trouble with you, always worrying about the damn furniture."

Dan wrote Mickey a letter the day he took her to court to try to prove that she committed adultery with their dearest old friend of forty years who had since passed away from lung cancer. Thank God the judge knew enough to throw his case out. The letter promised no more physical or verbal abuse. What a farce that was. She called him on the phone and tried to talk to him because he committed perjury in court. She later went to his apartment and asked him to make her a cup of tea and to try to talk things over. It ended up with him throwing her around and twisting her arms, which ripped the muscles in her back, giving her muscle spasms. She went home and laid on ice packs until the next day. She went to the doctor, got a written report for physical therapy, and also sent a report to her lawyer. The case is still pending. Mickey had back surgery six years ago, which didn't turn out well. She was also rear-ended while her car sat at a stop sign one year ago.

Dan went to Mickey's residence with a wrecking bar and knife. He ripped open windows on the garage, threatened her with a knife when she tried to stop him, and smashed the shadow man she had recently made and put on the garage. He threatened to kill her three brothers if they tried to protect her from him. The law says they can't do anything until he does something worse.

There is a picture of Dan giving his daughter away at her second wedding. It is weird the way the copy machine made it look like a book. Mickey thinks it is God's work. What a story lurks inside it. Looks like his little black book, doesn't it? The man calls himself a "bastard." That underestimates the truth. To add insult to injury, Mickey's lawyer tells her he has a vivid imagination which is why he accuses her of being with other men; a sick mind is more like it. This is not a figment of her imagination. It is all a true story. Mickey has made cassette tapes of their conversations to prove her story; however she hasn't been allowed to play them. Why?

Dear Lee,

I don't want to hear how you have Grandma in your heart anymore. Every time I come to your house I see the things you decided to take out of her house the day after she died. I didn't know she was dead until I got to Mar-Mac Dairy. Lorey said she was sorry to hear about my mother when I went in there to pick up a quart of milk. It was a human mistake. It could have been either one; anyhow, I told her it probably was Dan's mother. What a hell of a way to hear it. You didn't allow me to get my feelings out that day.

I went to visit her one day. She told me you had been there and spoke for her wooden rocker. She cried every time I went to visit her. She wanted to know why Dan didn't come to visit her. I told her I didn't know and that she would have to ask him. He treated her as you have been treating me. Every time we took her on a trip with us, he had his nasty mouth on her. He didn't want to visit her when she had her broken hip. He told me I made him do things he didn't want to do. I don't know why he felt that way.

I went down to see her before we left for Tom and Eddie's for Thanksgiving. I asked her if she wanted me to come and get her in the hospital, but she said no. She wanted at least another week in her home. I respected her wish. She wouldn't eat the food that Jane took her unless I stayed and ate with her. Before we left, Kent told me to tell his brother to get off his ass. That wasn't up to me. That's between them. They always get me in the middle of their shit. I told Dan, "Go to your brother." He refused.

When Grandma U. was coming home from the hospital, after she broke her hip, Jane told me that she didn't want her in her house. She told me that when I walked down to her house. Dan asked me if he should go down and spend the night; he shouldn't have had to ask me. He should have known where he should be. He went into a deep depression after her death. You didn't see it. I did. Guilt, I assume.

I didn't want anything from the will. He told me when I came up from the barn that if that's how you all felt we would go through it together. Wrong! He went to work. I told him to go get the red and white carnations and put them on the alter. You and Jane both used your vicious mouths on me that day. Neither of you had enough thought to apologize or consider my feelings. I didn't want a chipped lemon squeezer or the gold glasses. That was real generous of all of you. Jane told me she didn't want her in her house the day we walked down to see you—ask her if you don't want to believe me—I couldn't give a shit. I didn't want Grandma's freezer. It was left up to me to dispose of it. I went up to Grandma Guard's crying. She asked me if I was afraid of you—not you, Lee—you had already used your mouth on me, prejudged.

To read a will without Dan present; that was wrong. He was her son. He should have been present at the reading of the will. Being the executor did not give you the right or whoever made the decision. If you read the will right you would have seen. It said Kent and Dan were to share and share alike her possessions. That should have been between Dan and Kent. An executor is only to see that things are done as the will reads. Grandma had asked me to be her executor when I was there one day, but I refused. I saw what it did to Dan and Kent's relationship when Clarence died. The reason she asked me is that we had talked many times and she knew my thoughts. The will goes as it reads. The reason Kent didn't talk to Dan for a number of years was that he was worried that he would not receive the house she lived in. He treated Grandma like a piece of shit after Clarence died. He called her up and screamed at her at least once a week. She would call me up crying. We'd go to lunch to help her through it. She called me up one day and asked me to come down. I don't remember what year it was; that is immaterial. She wanted me to have some of her cut glass. She wanted to make sure I got the blue fluted dishes. We knew each other very well. I shared a lot with her. Clarence went behind her back and called Jane. He told her she better get down there or she wouldn't get anything.

Candy asked me the story behind the blue dish one time when we were talking. The beautiful one that sits on my hutch. It was given to Grandma on her sixteenth birthday. She wanted me to have it to cherish. It was meant to be. It has been very precious to me. It is a daisy and plum pattern, carnival glass. I went to the library because I was curious. I had thought I might pass it down in the family and wondered about who of all of you would cherish it as much as I have. My family's actions now and through the years make that a difficult decision.

You, Lee, have used your mouth on me when I was in Erie County Medical Center. Remember how you told me he (Dan) had wasted the last twenty years of his life on me? The counselor I saw in there told me, good for me—that I told you it wasn't good for you or me. Nice going, every time there is a crisis in our family you decide you have the right to run things, hurting me or anyone that gets in your way. I heard a snotty remark you made when you and Ray left the hospital room. I saw you look down your nose at me at Dan's retirement party. You're playing the same dirty games Dan did, aren't you? Like I told your husband the other day when he returned the keys to this house, "If this isn't resolved before Dan or I die, you have laid one hell of a number on yourselves." You have no right to judge how I feel. I know Dan much better than you do, but you all have to live with yourselves.

You wrote a letter to me when I was in Charleston; you couldn't even let me have a vacation without bringing up some old personal hurt, could you? I question that you care anything about my feelings. I call it very bad timing on your part. I went there to get a rest away from your mouth. Dan's dirty name for me is what he has to live with. The last thing you called me was "egotistical bitch." You set out to break up our marriage a long time ago. Now you have won. He didn't want me to listen to you. You really expect me to have a better life now than I had three months ago? I don't see any of you taking the physical burdens or financial stress off my mind right now. If you would have taken the time to come into the house the day you dropped off the dog crate, you would have seen I had raisin-filled cookies waiting for you. Better that I give them to someone who appreciates them.

Now when Grandma Guard was dying, I didn't want you and Teresa at the funeral parlor when you came. The worst was over. Watching her suffer was very painful; I loved her very much. I wanted to be there for her when she died. I don't regret it. The good is coming out of the bad from Grandma Ulrich's funeral and the way you all threw your guilt on my shoulders. Your children picked up from your actions on me. Now they think that is the way they should treat me. Bad teachings, Lee! Jane just told me two days before I had my breast biopsy done this summer, she was overdosed with chemo.

Debbie and you have had your heads and mouths on me for a long time. She came to visit me once when staying at your house. She wanted some relics from the shop and barn. She said she would pay me for them. I didn't care what she took. I wouldn't have accepted anything for them. "I'll bet your mother has a lot of nice things at her house," she remarked. Don't you think I know what she wanted? It's not up to you or any of you to judge that situation either. You think it's terrible what she did, too. Grandma Guard knew how people came in to grab what they thought they had the right to; she talked about it many times.

If you have the nerve, go ask Jane if she didn't just tell me. She decided to tell me two days before I had the lump removed from my breast this last summer. Grandma Guard was overdosed with chemo. I hung up on her; that was bad timing. You are always ready to judge me and my actions, aren't you? Right now I don't believe you are one bit concerned about whether I live or die. Keep up your viciousness on me. You may get your wish.

The true thing I told Lena the day she came into the trailer was that she's not going to take over where you left off. I didn't push her into the wall, which would be the same nasty habit you have. You can't blame anyone for that but yourselves; the fact is that you allowed her to act the way she did to me. It is a disgrace, but you applaud that kind of behavior. I question how any of you sleep at night. Roy Sr. had the nerve to make fun of the help I hire and what we are doing here. I feel sorry for all of you.

The Christmas party you had Sunday must have been joyous. You got your way, didn't you? Go on down to Sheila Bunner's and brag how you treated your mother. They know the hurt I had that day. I've been there to visit several times since George towed the trailer. I like their horses. Go see them and brag how you spent your Christmas hurting your mother. They heard some of the crying. I'm glad now I went where I did on Christmas Eve and Christmas Day. I was allowed to be myself. I wasn't criticized; I wasn't judged for every word out of my mouth. I was asked to come back. You have been on your pedestal for quite some time, just as Dan was. Let me know when it crumbles out from under you. Feel sorry for Dan; he needs it. Listen to him cry his story. I'm sure you won't hear any good about me.

Cap and I may write a book. She has many chapters I've been sharing with her for quite some time. We named the book two weeks ago: *My Sister Has Lived a Nightmare*. If it becomes a movie and I live long enough, I told her I would be the star. I told her it's a best seller and that I still have a pretty good leg on me for sixty-two. And I don't mind showing it, the hurt from Dan's dirty accusations! I hope I get the chance to go all over a young man in the movie. I'll send Dan a video tape so he can watch and know what he lost. He may get to see my baggy tits and sloppy cunt and ugly face on the screen. Then he'll know where he was wrong to use his sick, dirty mouth on me. That came out the first time.

I have asked my lawyer to move the case up as soon as possible. Dan's lucky he got Christmas at your house. I had hoped it would have been all over with December 19. I didn't know it wasn't going to be until three o'clock that afternoon. I had talked to the assistant district attorney, Mike Pliska, and my attorney. None of them liked the evidence I have to present in court. It shows what I have been putting up with at home.

I'm not sure if I have to have Todd summoned to court to testify what went on in our house when he was spending the day with me. You ask Dan if he remembers what he did to me that day when he pushed me up against the kitchen sink and accused me of spending all of his mother's money. I asked him not to do that and act that way with Todd there. Todd wanted to stay with me that night to protect me. He was just a child, but I am sure he didn't forget it.

This is the rotten behavior Dan has to face in himself. Now you tell me to see a psychiatrist. The people I talk to want to know why I put up with this rotten bastard as long as I did. It was because I didn't believe in divorce. I thought it was more important to keep a family together. I was wrong. I should have brought it all out before you all told me what is wrong with me. Dan tells me that is what is wrong; the people I'm working with think it is right that I remember.

It's all coming to light no matter what. I'm not Grandma. I am not Grandma Guard. I'm not going to back down and cover any of this shit. You will all have to bear the disgrace in whatever way you choose. That's really all you are worried about now. It's going to hurt your pride and disgrace you. It's not a pretty picture. Dan thinks I'm trying to get even. I'm not! He doesn't want me to tell everything. I shouldn't have tried to cover and hide it as long as I did or take the burden all on my back.

I am only responsible for my actions; not any of yours. I can only change myself. I hope you will see the good and not only the bad side of this. I asked for moral support. Like I told Roy Sr., "If any of my children had the nerve to sit in the court room, I wouldn't have to defend myself to any of them. They would know."

As this all comes out, you've all been crying to me how bad your lives are. You've had a piece of cake. I hope none of you have the misfortune to walk in my shoes. I'm sure you would all have the answers regarding how you would have dealt with it. It's easy to make decisions for the other person. I've said that many times. This isn't a television soap opera. This is a real life story, and it's pretty damn soiled.

Do you want to get in the book and have a few chapters of your own? Cap might. She had some very similar episodes. Her story brought on a stroke which she will never recover from; I guess that's what you are planning for me. I may prove you won't get your way. If you do, you'll all have to live with it.

I talked to her last night. I think Teresa better write a letter of apology to her and to me for overreacting and spoiling Cap's vacation and causing me stress that I wouldn't have expected from her. If she chooses not to, then she has to live with her guilt. I did tell Cap not to hold her breath. Evidently the children I raised don't know how to apologize, and if they don't mean it, why bother? It will eat away at all of you as Dan's is doing to him. You can't take back wrong actions and dirty words. I'm told that by apologizing and forgiving we will be forgiven. It's human to make mistakes. Making amends and trying to work it out and making the same mistakes over and over is a lesson well learned. I thought children were adults at an earlier age than any of mine are now. Wrong!

The fact that you would all sit in your house and allow Lena to use her mouth on me and then have a party shows me you are about the most cold-blooded, heartless people I've every met. You are just plain ignorant of my feelings. It shows me that you have lost control over her, allowing her to act that way at her age. I feel sorry for Ryan being raised in an environment like he is. He doesn't stand a chance in hell any more than Roy Jr. does.

Mickey

The Beginning of the End

Dear Dan:

I went to see Mr. O'Malley on Wednesday. He told me that your lawyer is trying to get you in his office—mainly about legal support. You don't have the right to dole out what you think I should be able to live on. The law states you are going to have to support me at whatever level the court decides upon. You will have to pay or you will be hauled into court. They feel it is impossible to expect me to live on four hundred dollars a month; I know it is.

I ran into Anna Pamphrey at South Gate. She asked about you. I wouldn't have believed you would be the kind that would do this to your wife. I can't cover for you. The fact that I allowed you to use your dirty mouth on me for years is hard for many to understand. "Why did you put up with it for so long?" everyone asks me. I tell them that I didn't believe in divorce. Everyone asks me when am I getting my divorce, and I tell them the truth, that I had asked for six months space from you. I'd had hoped you would get help from counseling or from a psychiatrist on your own, for your own benefit. I knew you had mental problems when we went to visit Lois and Arnold the last time. I told you that when we were on our way home, that you either had physical or mental problems.

I stopped in to see Norman Gotbey this week. I had been sent to an arthritis clinic in Batania. I saw a woman doctor there. She confirmed that the pain in my lower back and spine was coming from arthritis and scoliosis. She asked me to try another medication to get some relief, but it has not given me much help so far.

She told me not to shovel snow or vacuum and that heavy lifting would aggravate it. She is sending me to a pain clinic at General Hospital, but she offered me no guarantees. Hope I can get some relief there.

She wanted to know why I had to do those things if I was married and if I had children and grandchildren. She wondered why I still had to shovel snow and put wood in a wood furnace. That just kept aggravating the physical period. (They also asked about my sex life.) Every doctor I saw asked me these questions. They want to know why you would expect me to mow lawns with this condition. I told them they would have to ask you. They want to know why you want to put me through such stress as you are now when we were supposed to be enjoying life. They want to know why I have to carry groceries up a hill and steps. Not a pretty picture, is it? They also want to know why you would try to deprive me of a house I waited for all my life? I tell them that if I say I hurt I get told I'm complaining and that if I cry that is not allowed. I guess my husband and family have to live with themselves. Let them explain. I don't make excuses for their actions, and I'm not going to. Then the next words out of their mouths are: "Your husband is depriving you of heat while he is in a heated apartment? He is using money for lawyer's fees which he could have paid your last heating bill with in order to keep the pipes from freezing. What's wrong with him?"

I have ripped out your sick room in the garage; I didn't want it there anymore. It was a constant reminder of your last few months. I have insulated the garage, and I also have heat on in the back entrance. I am also redoing the walls; you sure left me with a nice mess, didn't you? I hope it makes you feel proud of yourself. You always did like to pick on someone when they were down. Now everyone I talk to says you had planned this for some time. That is why you had to have a cellar put in, so you could sell it for a better price. I've made my decision on how to pay off this house.

I'd like my picture back that I gave you for Christmas as long as I don't turn you on. Cap and I are writing a book about my life. I want it for the book. We named the book last week, *My Sister Has Lived a Nightmare*. We have the cover done also. If it gets published, I hope you take time to read it. The last years of our lives together is the grand finale. It will probably discourage anyone from entering into a marriage.

A funny thing happened the other day. The sign in front of the house with your name on it came loose—the wind blew it toward

Cowlerville. You won't be able to blame me for that. It is just one of those things that no one can explain. I'm going to take a picture of it to put it at the end of the book. How is the fishing at Case Lake?

I went to our accountant Monday night. They and Mr. O'Reily will try to figure out the income tax. Mr. O'Reily asked me, "Mickey, are you still married?" I replied, "In name only and according to the law. I haven't had a husband for ten years. Dan told me I could have anything I wanted. This is his way of giving it to me."

Mickey in Her Younger Years

Weekends began with a lawnmower and moving cars to the back yard. All were awaiting their weekly baths and tune-ups inside the huge old homestead. Kid's heads poked out from warm beds and started the day bickering over who woke first. Mickey arose and wrapped herself in a blue robe and pinned her hair. The coffee pot soon sang its happy little tune and cinnamon rolls sent their fragrance out over the window sill. The lawnmower quit outside the door, and Tom bounded into the kitchen to get his father, who had come in for his breakfast and gathering with the kids. He mumbled casually to the family while munching sweets washed down with good coffee.

Dan and the kids talked over one another, making plans and requests for a lifetime. No one ever asked, "Mickey, what do you have in mind?" She planned to clean up the kitchen, make the beds, call Joyce, and would suggest, "Let's go out to Lablaw and get the sales." Then they could stop back at Ma's for lunch.

All deeds must be accomplished to be back on Centerline and be at Ma's by 11:30 A.M. She was busy snipping beans. Something was simmering on the back of the stove. There was never a time when she wasn't preparing food to eat. Having come out of the Depression when some didn't eat, the greatest fear was there would be nothing to cook. A warmth filled the room as well as Mickey's heart. She had grown up in that mother's care all of her life. Being smaller than most in the family, she stood straighter and talked louder than the rest. She had always picked her share of friends.

Back to Reality

It was an ordinary Saturday in Mickey's life. She bounced out of bed—whoops, one leg at a time, slowly, damn back, arthritis or whatever, rainy weather—and checked the black, Rosecomb bantee chickens. There was no lay. She would go out and feed Chelsis, the newly acquired dwarf goat who was surviving on oatmeal and water and eating her bedding of hay.

Candy,

I heard that the situation between you and Mrs. Wilson is better, but there is never any guarantees what the outcome will be. Now I am going to do the same. If you found it hard to believe that Todd wanted to come out to visit me, ask him. Allow him time to answer. Also I would like you to ask him what he witnessed when he spent the night at our house when you lived on Maple Hill Road. Ask him about Dan coming into the kitchen. Todd was watching TV at the time; it was when Dan backed me up against the kitchen sink, demanding to know where I spent all his mother's money. I asked Dan not to do that with Todd present. I offered to take Todd home after he left to go to work. He wanted to stay with me.

I had put a slide bolt on the stair door so that Dan could not come up and go after me. I also asked you to have Paul take him fishing, which he did, telling Dan I thought he was crazy. It all made matters worse, "Mickey, Paul told me you think I'm crazy."

He went into a deep depression after Grandma died. The mistake I made was to try to take it onto my shoulders. He would not seek help. He has been taking his sickness out on me. I've asked some of you to get him to a doctor. He admitted to me that he has a problem. I was concerned about him when I was in Charleston. He told me he doesn't know where to get help now. I offered to set up an appointment with a psychiatrist for him. He is refusing help.

As soon as my lawyer contacted his, he said he blamed me for everything. What else is new? It won't work. He has brought his problems on himself. The stories he is running around and telling you kids is more of his game to make himself look good. You can believe him if you want to; that is up to you. If he was concerned about any of you he wouldn't be creating a mess like he is. Now you can believe what you want to but I couldn't deal with his actions anymore.

The people I have been working with in domestic violence

since June told me if I followed through, it would take a while. Once he goes to jail, a psychiatrist would visit him. That is why I have not backed down. Also he will have to face himself and not blame anyone but himself. This has been going on in him for too long. Ray Sr. knows some of this. I shared it with him when I asked him to oversee the house when I was in the Cleveland Clinic. He doesn't know if he can accept it. I talked with my lawyer before I flew out there. I said that you are all going to have to accept it like I have. He said, "Yes, Mickey, they are."

I did not go to a lawyer to get a divorce. I went for advice on how to protect us financially. It was suggested that we try a six month separation, giving us both time to relax and make reasonable decisions. I have informed Ray Sr. that neither he nor Paul needs to make room in their barns for any of Dan's tools. They are marital property. The ones he has in his station wagon are also marital property. They don't belong to him. I allowed him the privilege of coming to the house to pick up one saw. Frank Sawyer was present; Dan stood in the driveway and told Frank I lived like a pig. It is quite evident that statement is not true. You can verify this if you care to.

I've had all the locks changed as he has been sneaking in here and removing things after I received the protection order. He has violated that order many times. That is a misdemeanor. That is what he has to face in court. It is up to the judge if he goes to jail and for how long. He brought this on himself. Physically abusing me is not allowed anymore either. I refuse to take his verbal abuse anymore. What he told me is that he would not talk in court anymore. I have also been taping his actions and conversations for quite some time. I had to do it for my own protection. This has all been shown to and heard by people I am working with. When we go to trial this is the evidence that will be shown in court.

He filled the sleeves of his new jacket with caulking compound; I found that when I was packing his clothes. I spoke with Dr. Ribella and made an appointment for him before I went to the Cleveland Clinic. I wanted to know if he was crazy. The doctor said that he could run brain scans and such on him to check him out. It might be Alzheimer's or hardening of the arteries, but someone has to take him there and find out. I'm not going to. He refuses any help from me.

He has ruined both of our lives and his reputation in Wales and in Cowlerville. The Brownwell delivery man wanted to know what was going on. I'm sick of explaining his actions to people.

He runs around telling people that I threw him out. The first sheriff I called asked him to leave. He said he didn't hear him. Wales has an open criminal court. I'm not spreading rumors on him. What he is doing is very evident and has been from the first night he appeared in court.

I didn't want to bring this out until he has had his retirement. He would have lost his job at the post office. Les Hensel said he noticed it the last couple of years that he worked there. I was told to confront him in public or anywhere I had to. It might shame him into getting help or acting like a decent man ought to act. Expose him in town court; don't cover up for him.

Other people have lower opinions of him for what he is putting me through. This is what he has to live with. He tells his lawyer that I hate him. I feel sorry for him, but I can't help him. They tell me to think of myself for a change.

I prefer that Paul would stay out of the situation and stop helping him find work as he is wasting his time. All he is doing for himself is—well, I'm not saying they are two of a kind; it's up to Paul what he does, but it doesn't speak well for him. It's like helping a little boy get away with his dirty work. I though Paul was a nicer person than that. I hope that I am not wrong. If this is the kind of example you want your boys to follow, you will know what to expect when they become men. Is this what you would like them to learn? I hope not.

I'm sure you know that Clarence tried to make out with me when Teresa was two months old—that's the same way Dan was acting. I've had black and blue arms. I was at Abbey's when Dan came in with a whiskey bottle; he wasn't drunk. He used his dirty mouth on me for the last time. Now he says like Clarence did, "You have to tell it all, Mickey." He wouldn't go to his father and tell him what he meant. He wants to make excuses for himself so he can go to bed with other women. He should look in the mirror at himself, and he would see what I see.

I used to laugh when we were younger; I let him get away with feeling Jane up. She got beat up the night he did it to her. Now he sits and lies and says he just talked to Jane. She told me he didn't. When I went to Buddy Barrett for counseling, she heard about it and already knew the story. She asked him to come in for a session and asked him if he thought he was some kind of Casanova. He never wanted to come back for another session. It was easier to say his wife had a problem.

He allowed me to have shock treatments when he played his

game with Ida Lindhelm, my best friend. That is why they moved. Now he says, "The trouble with you, Mickey, is you don't forget anything." He always says, "If you don't like it, there's the door."

Abbey and I did a lot of talking when she took care of me. She also saw the black and blue arms when I drove there the next day. She said, "You aren't going to let him get away with that are you, Mickey?" No, I'm not.

I have to get past the image of his face as he was sitting in that brown chair, saying "Don't turn the kids against me, Mickey." I already knew what he meant. He started shining his shoes, getting his station wagon washed, and brushing his teeth. He took the package of razors in the medicine cabinet out to the shop. He started going out nights when Cap was there. He was trying to con another woman into believing what a nice guy he was. The fact is that she is listening to him. He'll pull the same dirty shit on her that he has on me. He doesn't want to change. I can't change him. He'll go on making fun of Howard and Shirley Dontely and everyone like he did in the past. He'll go crying to his kids or looking for hugs and sex from his wife or anyone else that is stupid enough to get involved with him.

People in Wales remember Clarence, and a few weeks ago someone said to me that he was a sneaky little son of a bitch. Dan is carrying the same label. Only they say he always seemed like such a nice guy. Some sneaky little son of a bitch Clarence was. I happened to be the sucker that got Dan. He thinks I'm trying to get even. I'm not. I am not going to cover for him either. He calls himself a bastard. This is the man that Dan is now. He used his wife to sign a mortgage with him so he could stiff her and make some money. He told me I could have anything I wanted so that I could cover his dirty tracks. This is what counselors hear everyday.

This is the man you are teaching your kids to love unconditionally. People want to know if I will ever take him back. No! They always ask the wife when she finally doesn't want to hear the lies, when she exposes his dirt to other people. When he gets caught and can't face himself, he moves on to another woman. He wants a divorce so that he can use the same dirty tactics on the next woman. He usually finds a younger girl that will fall for the trap of marriage like his first wife did. He wants to be trusted. He wants his wife to hug him and tell him that it's okay to call her a fucking bitch after she has prepared his meals and done his laundry. She has forgiven him until she is fed up with trying to make excuses for him. He threatens to put her into a mental institution if she can't accept his rotten behavior. He doesn't want it brought to light; that would spoil the image he has portrayed to the outside world on his job.

This was your mailman, an East Aurora Post Office rural carrier. This is the man that had his retirement party given to him by his daughter Teresa at Bryncliff. He was suppose to share the money with his wife and didn't. His wife took him out and treated him to a strip steak dinner at the Greenhouse Restaurant. Now this is Dan represented in Wales criminal court; he is a father, grandfather, great grandfather, husband.

My lawyer tells me that I am still married. I say in name only. I have just written Dan's epitaph. This is the man about whom people ask me if we can't work it out. This is the man that people are taking out to dinner and treating so that he can continue his dirty, sick behavior. This is the man people excuse by saying that he is just the way men are. Dan says all men are alike. "You got one thing right, Mickey," he told me as one of his last remarks before he left. I don't have to believe him though, do I? He is the product of Clarence.

He told me one night that I would never do anything except talk. He was wrong. That's the night I called Jock Lowe and asked him why in hell I had to put up with Dan's actions, throwing and breaking things in the house after he took him to The Moose for a couple of drinks. It was the next night that I called Jock. Dan pushed the receiver down so I couldn't keep talking.

I called his friend Dale Colburn one night to ask him if he would come over. Sharon, Dale's wife, answered the phone. She yelled, "Dale, Dan has something for you to do." He had just thrown another one of his tantrums. A young friend of my son's happened to stop in and was going to leave so that he wouldn't get involved. I told him to leave. I'm not afraid of Dale Colburn or Dan. He decided to stay in case Dan got violent when he came in. I told him he wouldn't. He went into his room and slammed the door.

This is the kind of behavior I have been dealing with for quite some time, not just since retirement. The physical and verbal abuse in addition to throwing food has probably been going on for eight or nine years. It has been getting worse lately. He told me that he did not have sex with me because I didn't turn him on. He told me Pam tried to get him excited by letting her tit hang out when he was there working. She didn't turn him on. He wanted to know why I didn't wear my negligees to the door like other women. I didn't have to. I had a hard time keeping men's hands off me as it was. I certainly don't want to encourage them.

I believe a man should have as much self-control as a woman when they are married. Women don't like every man's hands on them. If they cannot control their actions that's their problem not mine. Dan has a way of flaunting our sex life in public, trying to embarrass me; that's pretty low. He makes nasty remarks about me if someone approaches us when we are out. Now he has become such an excellent liar. I can't tell when he tells the truth and when he lies. He has always had a split tongue. The older he gets the wider the split gets. Everyone bends the truth sometimes. Dan's lying has become too good. It is hard to tell what is truth and what is lie. You can do what you want. I don't have to follow. I won't take my husband's mouth, my children's mouth, my grandchildren's mouth, or my son-in-law's mouth. If you can't accept that, that's your problem.

I'm not very proud of your behavior toward me. Your games are not needed. At thirty-nine years of age I say grow up. Everyone says I've been too nice to all of you. I didn't like it when Connie stole from you. Why do you have that problem with your own child? I'm not going to hide my purse when I have a family dinner. It's in plain sight, and anyone that takes money from it will be dealt with. I think it's pretty damn rotten that grandchildren are stealing from grandparents today, that children are treating their parents with verbal abuse and older people with disrespect. You all know better. The one doing the accusing usually has the problem. Talking behind someone's back and making fun of others doesn't work.

I was raised by entirely different standards. I loved my mother; I did not ask her for money, and I did not abuse her with snotty remarks. She didn't need that. She raised seven of us on very meager means. She taught me to appreciate what I worked for—self-sufficiency. I'm waiting for the day you start mouthing off to Dan. I'm not your beating post.

I don't see how your generation is doing very well raising children. If you want help you must ask for it. That's good advice. My mother didn't have to ask. If she said her rug was dirty, I simply went and shampooed it for her. I didn't expect anything in return. It was an act of love. She deserved it, and she appreciated it.

You make remarks about Lena to me. Would you like me to go to Mrs. Warren and repeat what happened in my kitchen one morning? Your conversation with Karen about how she's hurting you and that you don't want your father in jail? He is going to be disciplined by people who won't accept his childish behavior, temper tantrums, and dirty mouth. Exposing him is one of the hardest things I have ever had to do. You will have to deal with it and accept it. You can't blame me. I didn't raise him; I just got the end product. Unfortunately you are one of his children. You will have to bear the disgrace the best you know how. You can learn from his mistakes or act like him. That is up to you.

Retired Into Hell

Now their youngest daughter has questioned her. Mickey crawled into bed with Dan one night, and the first thing he asked her before she initiated sex with him was, "Well, did you get it while you were there?" "No Dan, I didn't. Did you?" No, he was in a very sick depression. As she lay in bed afterwards she thought, "God am I responsible for this? Am I guilty?" No, it wasn't her. He brought it on himself. He really trusted her, didn't he? When she left New Year's Eve day she was faced with all the Christmas decorations to take care of. The first time she called home, Dan said, "Mickey, I got problems."

"What are they, Dan?" she asked, but she got no answer.

Mickey would sing while she was in Charleston, "Who's going to fill my shoes? The sun will come out tomorrow." Arnold was right, he said he didn't think so. Mickey considered him her brother. He was important and sure appreciated the house when she finished it. She was the first wife there.

They went to the Masonic Hall dance. Everyone was so nice. "Where did you find that beautiful doll?" they asked. It was music to her ears. Mickey had not heard anything very good in Wales for some time. She had already told him, "Don't make up any stories, Hubar." Mickey figures she's a prude, but she won't sleep in a dead woman's bed. They had worked on the benefit in Lois's name. Mickey a silent member; she did send money once in a while. It's ironic, Arnold ended up using it himself. While Mickey was there, she went out with realtors looking for a winter home. Boy, Mickey sure does expect faith in the family.

There are so many stages of life; one of the happiest for Mickey was when the kids filled the house. I guess—no, I don't guess—I know that people without children and family are the ones to feel sorry for. They keep searching for something, work or whatever, to fill those twenty-four hours in a day. We are the lucky ones—mothers, grandmothers, and great grandmothers. Those are the privileged ones. Not to know this would be sad.

"Oh how I hate to get up in the morning." It's just a song. Baking in the wood stove—the smell of bread and roast beef.

Those Were the Good Old Days

The funny thing is that the cover of the book is The Mystery House—often referred to as The Wolf House. Charles Wolf lived there; he was an old bachelor. It is one of those unexplained mysteries of life. The picture of Jake and Mickey taken in front of the tombstone was taken when my sister Mickey was about fifteen. Little did she know that day that the Wolf House would become her honeymoon cottage.

She was a "squatter"; chickens lived in it. She was pregnant and needed a place to live since marriage was the choice. She needed lots of soap and water to scrub the floors; she had to get chicken shit smell out of the house. As she cleaned out between the boards with Clorox, the beauty underneath started shining though. Then she had to varnish those boards. What looked like a chicken ranch became a neat little home. It was her castle. Mickey had no maternity clothes; just an old yellow plaid shirt to cover her body and jeans with elastic that would expand. The three-quarter sized iron bed, bought secondhand for five dollars was to become her place to rest her head.

Those were the good old days. She would fill the oil stove in the living room and open the front door to let the sunshinne in to warm the house. The wood stove would be burning in the kitchen, too. It was clean with a tiny bedroom upstairs.

Her husband came home drunk many times, and we would dive out the back window to vomit, knocking all her plants off the stand. He worked at the steel plant on the swing shift. He threatened to leave her. By then she was pregnant with the second baby, a mere six months after the first one. She was eighteen. The Doberman puppy got free from

Eddie the mailman and tried to bite Lee when she reached through the playpen. The dog left for a new home: The Society for the Prevention of Cruelty to Animals.

One of the days when the front door was open—solar heat in 1948, would you believe—a four foot milk snake came slithering into the house. As it slid past her into the kitchen, Mickey ran and grabbed a stove poker to kill it. Somehow the snake disappeared and couldn't get out the door as she had shut it. There was only one place that damn snake could be. Every time she laid down to rest on the old blue and gray couch with its lumpy cushions smelling of dust, it would creak and make funny noises. The damned snake must have enjoyed living in the coils, one of which would often jab her in the rear. Oh well, he died there, too; she found the skin later on. The hair would raise on the back of her neck, but she'd just shrug and doze for a few minutes, get up, and get on with her day.

During that time they had to carry water from the well in an aluminum pail, put it on the stove in a dish pan, and get it hot enough to wash the baby diapers. Mickey had no washing machine; just her two hands and no inside plumbing. What was called the bathroom was just a back house (a two seater) behind the chicken house. She always made sure she went out for the last time before dark.

Back to the present. There is a story behind this sign. In the winter of 1992 the marriage was at an end. Dan had taken up with another woman. He had mental problems, depression, and decided that he wanted a divorce. He was not happy. Mickey put on a wool plaid jacket and took pictures with her Polaroid camera, and the first pictures were hazy, snowy, and gloomy as her thoughts ran wild. She was capturing the sign that she and Dan had made together for their retirement home which was built in three months by working together. After the mortgage papers were signed, he asked for a divorce. She wanted the signature to show in the picture so she moved a little closer. The second picture was stormier than the first; it represented the problems in her life today.

How could a perfectionist take pictures that weren't turning out? Oh, that's why. See the sun in the picture? It was God's way of speaking to her: After the storm, the sun will come out tomorrow; the future looks much brighter. It's time to move on with her life. There is always a lull before the storm. Only time will tell; time will heal the ugliness. The sun will shine tomorrow: "Tomorrow Today will be Yesterday." You can't look back—just live today well and tomorrow will take care of itself. Whatever will be will be.

She'd face that after a good night's sleep. First she would say the mother's prayer, tuning out the kids' problems, and pray for the good and loved ones. A special prayer for Dan, wherever he was, would leave her with a feeling of contentment.

"You take care of it God; I'm tired. You're in control. I'm stepping down from my pedestal. He does a much better job when I allow Him to take over. I'm just an imperfect human being and glad of it."

Dear Dan,

This is a form letter to let you know we are still married in name only. Some people get just what they deserve, all in good time. Some get too smart or think they are. You have a problem: You think you are better than other people. Now I know better. Everyone has to climb their own mountain.

The only tears you shed are for yourself. I don't feel sorry for a man that throws Easter candy in his wife's face. That is sick. When you don't have money to buy Easter candy, you will have something to cry about. All your little games haven't worked. Maybe you have been outwitted. Eventually you will get caught. Want to try for more? Cheaters have to pay with their guilty consciences. Your insinuations are our problem.

Please don't bother writing letters to 5501 Merlau Road. Whenever the man who is looking for you finds you, he won't be fussy about whether your teeth are clean or dirty. That is why I don't get involved in triangles. You vented your anger. You married the wrong sister! When you hit Attica prison you will get your wish. You will also be on TV so enjoy your vacation there. You will be with your own kind. Why did you want a divorce?

Hope you didn't have a big party planned. The joke is on you—you did get an *A* in math, but I won the spelling bee. Where were you educated? Wales Four? Looking in shit house windows? You're a brain, or is it *B* for bastard?

That's right, Dan.

Live and Learn

Dear Dan,
Re: Fucking Bitch

How ironic. I am typing this on the typewriter that I loaned out, and it came back with broken keys. I got to pay the bill.

If you can't pay your rent, move out. Take you own advice.

Every time I listen to you or our children it was the biggest mistake I made. This is a good chapter for the book. It's called "Live and Learn". We should learn from our mistakes. It's called being a good politician; when someone says they aren't too smart, agree with them. Some people live in a fool's paradise. Some face reality. Eventually those who think they are smart make an asshole of themselves. Give them a little rope and the noose tightens. Different terms for different terds; or do you spell it turds? Oh well, maybe I mean to say, oh shit! Then I might as well say what I mean! Oh shit!

Paul called you a bastard. Ray called you a bastard. You called yourself a bastard. I agree with all of you. Work for the bastards; isn't that what men are like? They all are bastards. I thought a bastard was a child born out of wedlock! Would you like to go to the head of the class? Define hostile! The one saying it was the problem! We could always crown you the biggest bastard in Wales if that is what you want! Is it time for a slurp of whiskey? Does the truth hurt? It takes one to know one!

Love thy neighbor but not his wife. You didn't move far enough away! Eat dog shit. It looks the same as hash. You never know! If a good wife feeds the bastard well, his kind will become extinct!

The Death of A Marriage

The Grand Finale

This is the grand finale, a divorce after Mickey played the role of a good wife, but a good wife will get the invisible knife. It is time to call up the minister and make arrangements to have the divorce performed in the church, so all the hypocrites she sat by in church won't have to sneak around town asking if it was done. All are invited to put on their Sunday best and watch the marriage of Mickey and Dan dissolve after forty-four years.

This ceremony will be a first. One of Mickey's tapes will serve as the organist. As Dan and she go back up the aisle, the carpet won't be white. It will be tarnished and soiled with the tears, and the blood from broken hearts will be painted all over it from the years of unhappiness. The grief-stricken Mickey will carry wilted flowers as a monument of the wasted years of her life. It will be like a funeral.

Casting off her burdens, she will have straight shoulders. She will hold her head held high as the minister begins his sermon. What God had put together, the devil will unravel. Instead of a robe, Reverend Finish, with a pitchfork in his right hand, will wear a red suit. Everything will be the reverse of the traditional marriage. The children from this dysfunctional marriage will be dressed in ragged clothes. As Dan backs up the aisle to repent from his sins, he will give testimony of his sick selfishness, letting his children see the real Dan for the first time, as he bellows in his usual tone. Limping, Mickey will come in wearing red velvet slippers. She will expose the surgery scars to the world, to the judges who turned their backs on her pleas for help, to the neighbors that helped keep a sick man out in the world.

They can applaud their stupidity for getting involved at the wrong time. They will throw stones at the Indian woman. Those who live in glass houses should not throw stones. They should not gloat over driving a woman out of her home town, just like the whites did to the Indians. But history repeats itself even in the nineties.

This is the sickness of a society of crazy people with weak brains who refuse to change. There will be no tears because cold blooded vultures don't have pure hearts, only hearts of stone. Dan will spit slime at Mickey. He will be dressed in ragged cutoff jeans. He will bounce out of church on a pogo stick, showing no remorse. He will justify his disgrace to his whole family with his whiskey bottle. Slurping it, he will celebrate his victory. Because these idiots don't have minds of their own, they will all sympathize with Dan no matter what the circumstances are.

When they go to sprinkle the holy water, it will be angel dust. Mickey will transform into one of God's beautiful angels with her halo of glittering gold and a smile on her face. She will know well that she is far superior to the traitors she thought were her friends. The irony might open a few eyes. It certainly won't be the first failure in this church that Mickey was a charter member of for so many years.

A hearse will pull up with vertical blinds to take away the man that destroyed himself by his own wicked, underhanded schemes with his homosexual friends. *Poison,* Mickey's terminology for what drinking can do, will be written on the hearse. She will be dressed in the red and black teddy so Dan can scream at her baggy tits, sloppy cunt, and ugly face. Her dog will be at her side. One touch from Dan, and he will rip his balls off.

Mickey will undo the legchains wrapped around herself, marriage chains of control Dan used on her. Dan will watch with his mouth sealed with gray duct tape and his hands cuffed. He will not be able to hurt this beautiful woman any more. A line of fishhooks will be strung along the pews, and he will be asked to run his hands down them before leaving. Watching the miserly man in the mirror with his hands full of the money he deprived his wife, he will realize the root of all evil.

Mickey will try to move on, putting this ugliness behind her. She has already changed the name "House of Spite" to "Empty Arms Hotel." She tries to help other lost souls. Some are beyond help.

There will be thunder and lightening, but as the ceremony ends the sun will come out to wrap up a job well done. It will come out after the storm.

